Tales from Harborsmouth

ALSO BY E.J. STEVENS

Ivy Granger World

Ivy Granger
Urban Fantasy Series
Shadow Sight
Blood and Mistletoe
Ghost Light
Club Nexus
Burning Bright
Birthright
Hound's Bite
Tales from Harborsmouth

Hunters' Guild
Urban Fantasy Series
Hunting in Bruges

Beyond the World of Ivy Granger

Spirit Guide
Young Adult Series
She Smells the Dead
Spirit Storm
Legend of Witchtrot Road
Brush with Death
The Pirate Curse

Poetry Collections
From the Shadows
Shadows of Myth and Legend

Super Simple Guides
Super Simple Quick Start Guide to Self-Publishing
Super Simple Quick Start Guide to Book Marketing

IVY GRANGER PSYCHIC DETECTIVE

Tales from Harborsmouth

E.J. STEVENS

Published by Sacred Oaks Press
Sacred Oaks, 221 Sacred Oaks Lane, Wells, Maine 04090

First Printing (trade paperback edition), July 2017

Stevens, E.J.
Tales from Harborsmouth/ E.J. Stevens

ISBN 978-1-946046-04-8 (trade pbk.)

Printed in the United States of America

TABLE OF CONTENTS

PRONUNCIATION GUIDE

Pronunciations are given phonetically for names and creatures found in the Ivy Granger series. Alternate names and nicknames have been provided in parentheses. In some cases, the original folklore has been changed to suit the city of Harborsmouth and its environs.

Ailinn: ah-lynn
Aleya: uh-LEE-yuh
Arachne: uh-RAK-nee
Athame: ah-thaw-may
Banshee: ban-shee (Bean Sidhe, Bean Sìth)
Barguest: BAR-guyst (Bargheist, Black Dog)
Bean Tighe: ban tig
Béchuille: beh-huh-IL (Bé Chuille)
Bema: BEE-muh
Bheur: ver (like air)
Blaosc: BLEE-usk
Bogey: BOH-gee
Boggart: BOG-ert
Boitata: boy-TAH-ta
Brollachan: broll-ach-HAWN
Brownie: BROW-nee (Bwca, Urisk, Hearth Faerie, Domestic Hobgoblin)
Bugbear: BUG-bayr (Bug-a-boo, Boggle-bo)
Bwca: BOO-kuh (see Brownie)
The Cailleach: kall-ahk (The Blue Hag, Cailleach Bheur, Queen of Winter, Crone, Veiled One, Winter Hag)
Cat Sidhe: KAT shee or kayth shee (Faerie Cat, Cait Shith, Cait Sith)
Ceffyl Dŵr: keff-EEL dore (Kelpie King, Ceff)
Chir batti: CHEER bhut-TEA
Clurichaun: kloor-ih-kon (clobhair)
Cu Sith: KOO shee
Daeva: DAY-va
Demon: DEE-mun

Djinn: JIN
Draugr: DROW-ger
Duergar: doER-gar
Each Uisge: erk OOSH-kuh (Water Horse)
Elphame: EL-faym
Emain Ablach: EH-van ah-BLAH
Faerie: FAIR-ee (Fairy, Sidhe, Fane, Wee Folk, The Gentry,
People of Peace, Themselves, Sidhe, Fae, Fay, Good Folk)
Fear Dearg: far DAR-rig (The Red Man)
Fionn mac Cumhaill: FIN mac COO-will •
Forneus: FOR-nee-us (Demon, Great Marquis of Hell)
Fragarach: FRAG ah roch
Fuath: FOO-ah
Gaius Aurelius: GUY-us aw-REE-lee-us
Galliel: GAL-ee-el (Unicorn)
Ghoul: GOOL (Revenant)
Glaistig: GLASS-tig (The Green Lady)
Gnome: NOHM
Goblin: GOB-lin
Griffin: GRIF-fin (Gryphon, Griffon)
Grindylow: GRIN-dee-loh
Gwarwyn-a-throt: GWAR-win-uh-THROT
Gwynn ap Nudd: gwin-AP-need
Hamadryad: ha-ma-DRY-ad (Tree Nymph)
Harborsmouth: HAR-bers-MOUTH
Henkie: HEN-kee
Hippocampus: hip-po-CAM-pus
Hob-o-Waggle HOB-oh-WAG-gul (Brownie, son of Wag-at-the-
Wa)
Hy Brasil: HY bra-ZIL
Ignus fatuus: IG-nus FATCH-you-us
Inari: i-NAH-ree
Jenny Greenteeth: JEN-nee GREEN-teeth (Water Hag)
Kelpie: KEL-pee (Water Horse, Nyaggle)
Lamia: LAY-me-uh
Leanansídhe: lan-awn-shee (Lhiannan Sidhe, Leanhaun Shee,
Leannan Sìth, Fairy Mistress)
Leprechaun: le-pre-khan (leipreachán)
Loup garou: LOOP guh-ROO
Mab: MAB (Unseelie Queen)

Manannán mac Lir: MAH-nah-nahn mac leer
Mauthe doog: MOW-thee DOO
Melusine: MEL-oo-seen
Mermaid: MER-mayd (male Merman)
Merry Dancer: MER-ree DAN-ser (Fir Chlis)
Murúch: mer-ook (Merrow, Moruadh, Murúghach)
Nixie: NIX-ee
Nuckelavees: NOOK-uh-LAY-veez
Oberon: OH-ber-on (Seelie King)
Peg Powler: PEG POW-ler (Peg Powler of the Trees, Water Hag)
Peri: PER-ee
Pixie: PIK-see (Pisgie)
Pooka: POO-kuh (Phooka, Pouka, Púca, Pwca)
Redcap: RED-kap (red cap)
Roca Barraidh: ROH-ka BAR-rah
Saytr: SAY-ter
Selkie: SEL-kee
Shellycoat: SHEL-lee-cote
Sidhe: SHEE (see Faerie)
Succubus: SUK-you-bus (male Incubus)
Tech Duinn: tek DOON
Tezcatlipocan: tehs-cah-tlee-poh-cahn
Tir na nOg: TEER na NOHG
Tir Tairngire: TEER TEARN-geer
Titania: ti-TAY-nee-uh (Seelie Queen)
Troll: TROHL
Tuatha Dé Danann: tootha DAY da-NAN
Tylwyth Teg: TILL-with TEEG (Seelie Court)
Unicorn: YOU-ni-korn
Unseelie: un-SEE-lee
Vampire: VAM-pyr (Undead)
Will-o'-the-Wisp: WIL-oh-tha-wisp (Gyl Burnt Tayle, Jack o' Lantern, Wisp, Ghost Light, Friar's Lantern, Corpse Candle, Hobbledy, Aleya, Hobby Lantern, Chir Batti, Faerie Fire, Spunkies, Min Min Light, Luz Mala, Pinket, Ellylldan, Spook Light, Ignus Gatuus, Orbs, Boitatá, and Hinkypunk)
Ynis Afallon: un-NIS AH-fuhl-on
Yue Fei: yweh-fay

FROSTBITE

"What a beautiful cat, Miss Granger."

I frowned, but let the comment slide. I didn't have any pets, not unless you counted the dust bunnies collecting beneath my desk.

Jess "Jinx" Braxton raised a questioning eyebrow, but I shrugged. I didn't have anything helpful to share with my rockabilly business partner. The frail woman tottering along at Jinx's elbow either needed new glasses or she was nuttier than weresquirrel poop.

Mrs. Boyd wouldn't be my first loony client. Working for a client who sees things that aren't really there is an occupational hazard when you advertise as the city's best (and only) psychic detective.

Who was I to judge? One of my special talents is the ability to see through glamour. A lot of supernatural creatures use glamour to hide in plain sight, and my gift cuts through the glitz and glitter of vampire compulsion and faerie magic. It's not as fun as it sounds. I've seen things no human should ever see.

Second sight is a blessing and a curse.

Monsters walk the streets of Harborsmouth. If it slinks, slithers, flies, or oozes, I've probably had the dubious pleasure of making its acquaintance. The fact that some of those things cross the street to avoid me hasn't escaped my notice. A detective's job is to take note of the little things, the small details that can break a case wide open, but having anthropomorphic snot treat you like you smelled worse than a troll fart could give a girl a complex. Some things are best to ignore or chalk up to sunny disposition.

I gave our client my best smile and waved a gloved hand at the seat in front of my desk. She flinched and latched onto Jinx's tattooed arm, huddling like a gryphon chick beneath its mother's wing. My partner shot me a warning glare and I toned down the charm.

"So, what can we help you with, Mrs. Boyd?" I asked, leaning back in my chair.

Best not to scare the client, at least not before she paid. Jinx reminded me of that often enough, and she kept the books. If she said we were in the red, then we were hemorrhaging our last pennies. Magic weapons and protective spells don't come cheap, and Jinx complains when we run out of food. So, I rested my gloved hands on the desk where my client could see them, adopted a relaxed pose, and tried not to let the woman's cat comment stir up painful memories of my childhood pet. Fluffy was dead and there was no sense living in the past. Surviving in the present was hard enough.

"Please, call me Maggie," she said, taking a seat.

Mrs. Boyd, Maggie, cast a nervous glance toward Jinx. I sighed, but nodded for Jinx to stick around. It looked like we'd be working this case together.

The fingers on my right hand reflexively went to my forearm, checking and double-checking the comforting presence of the silver-tipped iron blade hidden beneath my leather jacket. Something had our client spooked and Jinx was the people person in our little business venture, but having my partner leave the office set my teeth on edge. She was organized, great at keeping me on track, and sweet as cherry pie to our clients, but my partner had a knack for personal injury. We didn't call her Jinx for nothing.

"Okay, Maggie," I said. "How can we help?"

I held my breath, trying not to fidget in my chair. Maybe this would be an easy case, something completely mundane. Not every case was fraught with danger. Jinx might finally make it through a case without bumps and bruises.

So why were my insides being torn up by a pack of rabid vampire bats?

"It's my house," she said, waving her hands. Her cheeks flushed and her over-bright eyes darted between Jinx and me. "It's haunted."

That was doubtful. There are a lot of weird things that exist in Harborsmouth. I knew that more than most. But I'd never seen a ghost.

I put on my best poker face, leaned forward, and made a show of picking up a pen and flipping open my notepad.

"Can you describe this ghost?" I asked.

"Oh, the place is quite haunted," she said. "There's more than one ghost. I'm sure of it."

"And what makes you say that?" I asked.

"Furniture moving, moaning, groaning...that sort of thing," she said, blinking rapidly.

Jinx mouthed "pooka orgy?" from over Maggie's shoulder, and I had to stifle a giggle. My lip twitched, but I'd learned the hard way not to act like a crazy person in front of the clients, not until the check cleared.

"Have you noticed anything missing?" I asked, pen tapping a blank sheet of paper. "Spoons? Candleholders? Jewelry?"

"Nothing like that," she said, shaking her head.

Well, that ruled out Jinx's pooka orgy theory. I'd worked a few pooka infestations, and the supernatural rodents were notorious for stealing anything shiny that wasn't nailed down with iron. The only thing the bacchanalian critters liked more than an orgy was thievery.

"You're sure?" I asked.

"No, the only thing I've lost is weight," she said. "Which is strange since I'm hungry all the time. Not that I'm complaining. I was carrying around more than a few extra pounds before moving here last month."

That was hard to believe. The woman was gaunt to the point of emaciation. I narrowed my eyes and turned my head, trying to see through any lingering glamour. Most of the time, my gift works on its own, whether I want it to or not, but sometimes it needs a nudge.

"You moved here recently?" I asked, making a show of taking notes.

Sneaking up on the truth works in tricky cases, but all I saw in my peripheral vision was a frail woman in need of a sandwich. Something strange was going on here, and I had a bad feeling that I'd have to use my psychic gift before this case was solved.

You see, I'm twice cursed. Not only do I have the gift of second sight, a gift I'd happily return, but I also get visions when my skin touches certain objects. During a vision, I slip into a memory and experience events through the eyes of whoever left a psychic impression behind. The trouble is, it takes strong emotions to leave behind a psychic impression, and most things that make a person feel that deeply are painful or terrifying. Experiencing that much fear isn't healthy, and there was a very real risk of losing my sense of self, becoming trapped in someone else's nightmare, but sometimes it was the only way to solve a case.

Psychometry was a dangerous gift, but it paid the bills.

"Were there any belongings left behind by the previous owners?" I asked, chest tightening. "Or any rooms that weren't fully renovated before you moved in?"

"Oh, yes," Maggie said. "I've barely touched a thing. I had big plans for the place, but I haven't felt up to a big D.I.Y. project yet. I just haven't had the energy. And there are the ghosts to think of. Will you look into the matter? I know it's a strange thing to investigate, but when I asked around, everyone said that you're the one to handle weird...unusual cases."

I gritted my teeth, but nodded. I'd always been an outcast, a weirdo. Screaming about monsters and slipping into unwanted visions had led to a lonely childhood until I'd met Jinx.

"I'll take the case, but I need to investigate your house, go through some of the previous owner's old things," I said.

"Of course," she said, clutching her handbag to her chest. "Is today too soon? It's just...I haven't been sleeping. At least, I don't remember the last time I slept."

"No problem," I said. "Jinx has the address?"

She nodded, and I pushed away from the desk and stood. We had an active case and I didn't want to waste time, but it would be foolish to run off without a plan. My eyes flicked to the wall clock.

"Expect us around two o'clock," I said. "You're welcome to go out while we investigate. Just leave the door unlocked."

That gave us over an hour to come up with a plan and stuff my pockets with weapons and protective charms. I'd like more time, but the woman was visibly shaken. Whatever had invaded her home was drawing her energy in some way. She was practically fading out of existence as we spoke.

"Thank you, Miss Granger," she said, already standing and scurrying toward the door. "And don't worry about me being home. I retired just before moving to Harborsmouth, and I hardly ever leave the house."

Maggie Boyd walked out onto the streets of the Old Port Quarter, and I frowned. She was so sickly and rail thin, I'd mistaken her for an elderly lady, but the woman was only recently retired and more likely in her sixties. So much for my keen observational skills.

"Buck up," Jinx said with a wink. "So what if we have a reputation for taking on whacked cases? I say bring it on, the stranger the better. Weird is the new cool."

That was easy for her to say. Jinx hadn't seen the creatures that roamed our city, stalking humans as prey and ensnaring them in a deceitful web of pestilential lies and poisonous bargains.

I shrugged and opened the desk drawer where I kept my stash of hardcore protection charms. We were once again heading into unknown territory with no clue of what we were up against. Jinx could go on thinking a weird case like this was cool, but I listened to my gut, and right now my insides were churning into painful knots as my stomach tried to climb out my ear.

I was good at finding the truth, but I had a nagging suspicion that Maggie's house wouldn't reveal its secrets without a fight.

*****

Maggie Boyd's new digs were in a neighborhood to the north of the Old Port Quarter, wedged between the slums of Joysen Hill and the gentrification of the Quarter. There was a lower ratio of bars to homes here, but the streets weren't entirely residential. I would have missed the dead-end lane entirely if it wasn't for the kids using the sign for target practice. Their ammunition was broken chunks of pavement, but I gave them a smile with too many teeth, and they scattered.

We made it partway down the alley before the gang tags stopped and the brick buildings ended, replaced by a truck graveyard on one side of the street and a weed-strewn lot on the other. At the end of the lane, stood a simple house that had seen better days.

The house was a basic single-story Cape with faded clapboards that might have been red at one time, but now gave the appearance of flaking rust. A chain-link fence and the backside of a warehouse rose behind the structure, leaving the house in deep shadow. The alley was also dark, making the yard in front of the house the only sunny spot. Weeds, grass, and tangled vines thrived in the patch of sunlight.

"She has her own secret garden, cool," Jinx said with a grin.

"So did Miss Havisham," I muttered.

I eyed our exits before approaching the house. Maggie hadn't lived here long, but it was still surprising that the exterior and grounds were this rundown. If I didn't know better, I'd have guessed the place abandoned for decades.

I stepped gingerly over bits of debris, boots crunching on gravel as I made my way slowly down the footpath. The gate was gone, rotten away or scavenged for firewood, but my skin tingled as I passed beyond the dilapidated wooden fence and into Maggie's dooryard. A chill ran up my spine and I spun on my heel, but whatever I'd sensed, I was too late.

Jinx let out a startled cry, arms windmilling in an attempt to stay upright, but her platform sandals weren't helping. She reached out a hand, and I jerked away. It was a reflex born of years of negative visions, but I knew I'd screwed up.

As if Jinx's look of hurt and resignation wasn't bad enough, I overcorrected and landed on all fours. Warm wet grass slid inside the gap between my sleeve and glove, as if the ground was hungrily running its many tongues along my wrist, tasting my skin.

I shuddered, yanking my hand away and rapidly climbed to my feet. I'd had a run-in with Hunger Grass on a previous case and it hadn't gone well. In fact, the case had gone to Hell in a handbasket of woven rusty razorblades.

I rubbed gloved hands against my pants, and shuddered. Backpedaling, I glanced left and right, but nobody was trying to eat our faces off. It was just Jinx and me.

"What the heck just happened?" Jinx asked, frowning. "You get a vision?"

"Not a vision," I said, voice shaking. I swallowed hard, attention shifting to the house as I stepped back onto the path. "Our client ever mention an unexplained hunger or neighborhood pets going rabid?"

"No," she said, brow wrinkling.

"You sure?" I asked.

"I'd have remembered pets foaming at the freaking mouth," she said. "What gives?"

The correct question was, what takes? Hunger Grass was nasty stuff. Most people who step on a patch of the stuff end up changed and not for the better. First you lose your sense of right and wrong. Then you lose everything and everyone you ever loved.

I was immune to the stuff, but I had no idea why and even less interest in finding out. I'd hoped to never encounter that kind of magic again. No such luck.

"Our client has a patch of Hunger Grass in her front yard," I said, glancing at Jinx. "You know what that means."

She did. Jinx went pale, eyes widening.

"Oh shit," she said.

Oh shit was right. Hunger Grass was extremely dangerous. Most faerie magic is. But it takes more than just magic to create the slavering circle of weeds.

Something bad happened here, really bad. Like famine or a hard Maine winter driving a family to cannibalism bad.

"You think there are actually ghosts in there?" she said. I had to hand it to my partner. Her face was ashen, but she didn't run away. "The ghosts of eaten people."

"I don't know," I said, squaring my shoulders. "But we're going to find out."

The crunch of gravel beneath my boots punctuated my words and I tried not to think about trudging over bones picked clean of flesh. I barely twitched when Jinx rapped on the door, announcing our arrival.

We didn't have to wait long. The door swung open and Maggie stood there, eyes appearing sunken in the dim light. Had she touched the Hunger Grass? Was she infected with its magic?

"Please, come in," she said. "I'll be in the kitchen if you need anything. Don't leave without coming back for tea. The kettle's almost ready."

I stepped inside the house, a polite refusal on my lips, but gasped. The shabby living room fell away, revealing a horror so great I was at a loss for words.

This is not at all what I expected.

"What do you see?" Jinx asked, sidling up to me as our host passed through what I assumed was the kitchen door. "Looks normal enough."

"You don't want to know," I said, swallowing bile.

The walls were slabs of pulsating meat and the floor was sticky beneath my combat boots. I winced at the moist fetid air that hung heavy with the distinctive stench of a slaughterhouse. Fear and blood permeated every fleshy crevice, but over the underlying terror loomed a hunger that threatened to devour us whole.

"Jinx, go outside," I said, voice hard.

"Outside with the creeptastic Hunger Grass?" she asked.

She had a point.

"Fine, but keep close to me," I said, lowering my voice. "Stay away from the walls and don't touch anything. Assume that nothing in this house is what it seems."

"That's not very reassuring," she muttered.

"Good," I said, palming my knife. "If you're scared, we might just get out of this alive."

"What about Maggie?" Jinx asked.

A tapping came from the kitchen, and I stilled. Tap, tap-tap, tap. There was an agonizing pause before the tapping began anew. As much as I'd love to run screaming from this bizarre charnel house, we had a case to solve and a client to rescue.

"We're going to accept that cup of tea and find out what the hell is going on in this house," I said.

"And if it's a trap?" she whispered.

"We'll cross that bridge when we come to it," I said.

I just hoped that if we did encounter a bridge, it wasn't made of oozing muscle tissue.

On my signal, Jinx pushed open the kitchen door. At least, she swore it was a wooden door. If we made it out of here alive, I'd need a gallon of brain bleach to scrub that orifice from memory.

I gasped, staggering forward, but abruptly froze as my eyes darted back and forth from Maggie to the corpse wearing her clothes. Corpse might be too kind a word. The body was missing parts and had been gnawed on by more than rats.

That wasn't the scariest thing in the room, not by a long shot.

I'd located the source of the tapping. Two children huddled on the floor, their knobby knees and the jut of their collar bones painful to witness. They leaned into each other in a one-armed embrace, teeth chattering against a cold I couldn't feel.

"You can see them, can't you?" Maggie asked, voice hopeful and eyes pleading.

"She doesn't mean the bones on the floor, does she?" Jinx whispered from where she stood at my back.

"No, Jinx," I said. "But those bones are important. I'd put money on it."

In fact, the corpse huddled around the children's tiny forms, giving them comfort, even in death.

"Can you help them?" Maggie asked.

I glanced from Maggie to the body on the floor, and took a deep breath. I lifted my eyes to the children, turning my head to use the full strength of my second sight. The children flickered, but I caught a glimpse of rows of needle-like teeth, too many teeth for their gaunt faces.

Tap, tap-tap, tap. The chattering continued, and I winced.

"What...what did you do?" I asked.

"What any good mother would do, or so I thought," she said. "I eased their suffering. I kept them alive. I didn't know what would happen to them."

I was going to ask what she meant, but my mind finally caught up with what my eyes were seeing. They didn't have mouths ringed red and sticky from berry preserves and the youngest wasn't holding a doll to her chest. The little girl stroked a clump of her mother's hair.

"You were starving," I said.

Maggie nodded, eyes never leaving her children.

"They were excited for the snow, at first," she said. "It came late that year, but it more than made up for its tardiness. The winter was never-ending. And for them, it never will end. Not without your help."

"What can I do?" I asked.

"Tell them that they are good children," she said. "They did what they were told. They mustn't suffer for my evil act."

I frowned, but stepped forward and crouched down, careful not to touch the body at my feet. Being cannibalized was one vision I sure as hell didn't want to get sucked into.

"Ivy, what are you doing?" Jinx hissed.

What was I doing? I looked at the children, using my second sight to see every detail. Their teeth wasn't the only unnatural anomaly. Vein-like tendrils connected the children to the fleshy cabinets and gelatinous floor.

"Maggie's children are tethered here," I said, replying to Jinx.

I glanced up at Maggie, searching her face for clues. Her eyes were wide, but she leaned forward.

"Is that why they couldn't move on?" she asked. "Can you...?"

"I'm no expert," I said, cutting her off. "But from what I see, this house is feeding on the children's suffering. If I'm right, it might not like us removing its food supply."

"Is this a bad time to mention I'm not really dressed to battle a haunted house that feeds on the suffering of dead kids?" Jinx asked.

"Wishing you'd taken your chances with the Hunger Grass?" I asked.

"Hell, yes," she said. "But you're not leaving, are you?"

"Hell, no," I said.

"Fine, but, for the record, I'm totally cool with you losing your weirdo street cred," she said.

"What happened to the stranger the better?" I asked.

"Our client is dead, the house is alive, and there's grass in the yard with the ability to create ravenous wendigos," she said. "That's what happened."

I'd been watching the children while Jinx rambled. They didn't respond to Maggie or Jinx, but I could have sworn their eyes slid to me more than once. Maybe my second sight allowed some creatures to see me more clearly.

"My name is Ivy Granger," I said. "What's yours?"

They didn't reply, but both children turned their heads my way, unblinking. A low growling rose from their stomachs, and they stared at me with a feral gleam in their eyes. At least I had their attention.

Fear slithered along my spine and my glance darted around the room. Did Maggie invite us here to bring her children peace or dinner? I had to try to rescue the kids no matter my client's motives.

"I'm a friend of your mom's," I said.

Walls spasmed and red tears ran in rivulets down the children's cheeks.

"Ivy, did you feel that?" Jinx asked.

"Stay there and don't move unless I say so," I said.

Predators chase their prey. And these two stopped being innocent children long ago.

"Your mom is here and she loves you very much," I said. "You've been very good, but she needs you to do one more very hard thing."

"B-b-bad," the boy said.

"No, you're not," I said.

"H-h-hungry," the little girl moaned.

"You don't have to ever be hungry again," I said. "You can move on and be with your mom again."

I had no idea if what I said was true, but words have a magic of their own and there were strong energies in this house.

I tapped into my own sense of emptiness at losing a parent, a hole in the pit of my stomach and an ache in my chest that would never go away. I channeled a child's yearning for their parents and told the ghost children what they needed to hear.

They were good. They were loved. They were going home.

The more I talked the more convinced I was that I could save them. And just like that, a door opened and the children turned to face my client.

"Mommy?"

"Take my hand," Maggie said, reaching for her children. "We're going home."

The room shuddered, and Jinx lost her balance, but I kept my eyes on the children and the veins that tethered them to the house.

"We were bad," the girl said.

"No, my beautiful precious boy and girl," Maggie said. "You did exactly what your foolish mother asked of you. Can you forgive me?"

They ran to her, and as they reached the end of their fleshy chains, I sliced the veins with my blade. The knife was silver-tipped iron and sprinkled with holy water. I had no idea what the house was, but the veins blackened and withered, retracting with lightning speed.

Maggie mouthed "thank you" over the children's heads and stepped through the glowing door.

I heard her voice through the light, calling out in a cheerful voice.

"Come on, Fluffy," she said. "Time to go home."

Something brushed my leg and purring filled my ears. Then it moved away and the door snapped shut.

My ears popped and Jinx frowned.

"Was that a cat?" she asked.

I blinked away tears.

"I don't know, but I don't think we'll be getting paid for this job," I said.

Jinx looked around the dusty kitchen and groaned. The house was once again a mundane structure, the only oddities were the three bodies resting in each other's arms.

"We're never going to see a dime," Jinx said, staggering to the door.

The light was painfully bright, but I tilted my head to the sky and shrugged.

It's hard to pay the bills when you're dead. But if you die in a city filled with random faerie magic and have Ivy Granger on the case, you sure as Hell can settle your debts.

BLOOD AND MISTLETOE

INTRODUCTION

Welcome to Harborsmouth, where monsters walk the streets unseen by humans...except those with second sight.

Whether visiting our modern business district or exploring the cobblestone lanes of the Old Port quarter, please enjoy your stay. When you return home, do tell your friends about our wonderful city—just leave out any supernatural details.

Don't worry—most of our guests never experience anything unusual. Otherworlders, such as faeries, vampires, and ghouls, are quite adept at hiding within the shadows. Many are also skilled at erasing memories. You may wake in the night screaming, but you won't recall why. Be glad that you don't remember—you are one of the fortunate ones.

If you do encounter something unnatural, we recommend the services of Ivy Granger, Psychic Detective. Co-founder of Private Eye detective agency, Ivy Granger is a relatively new member of our small business community. Her offices can be found on Water Street, in the heart of the Old Port.

Miss Granger has a remarkable ability to receive visions by the act of touching an object. This skill is useful in her detective work, especially when locating lost items. Whether you are looking for a lost brooch or missing persons, no job is too big or too small for Ivy Granger—but you may be on her waiting list for awhile. Hopefully, you are not in dire need of her immediate services. After her role in recent events, where she was instrumental in saving our city, Miss Granger's business is booming.

If matters are particularly grim, we can also provide, upon request, a list of highly skilled undertakers. If you are in need of their services, then we also kindly direct you to Harborsmouth Cemetery Realty. It's never too early to contact them, since we have a booming "housing" market. Demand is quite high for a local plot—there are always people dying for a place to stay.

Happy holidays!

CHAPTER 1

I woke to the smell of gingerbread and coffee. Too bad the two were one and the same.

"This is why I hate the holidays," I muttered into my cup. "Who messes around with a perfectly good cup of coffee?"

"You're just grumpy because Ceffyl stood you up last night," Jinx said.

"Well, it was a lame excuse," I said.

I dropped my gloved hands into my lap, staring through a sheet of sleep mussed hair at the snowmen that danced maniacally around my pajama pants. I was pouting. Damn, I never pout, but I had been excited about our date last night. Which in retrospect was silly—I hate Christmas.

But this was my first holiday season with a boyfriend and I had wanted to do all of the normal date stuff. Instead, I sat home and watched Rudolph the Red-Nosed Reindeer for the gazillionth time. Jinx had suggested wearing the Christmas pj's we'd exchanged as gifts last year. I traced the smiling snowmen with a gloved finger, wishing I could be that happy for once.

Ceff had promised to take me to the tree lighting in Fountain Square. I didn't like crowds, and usually avoided them like the plague, but Ceff had lured me with promises of hot chocolate and my weight in peppermint cookies. He also said he had a present for me.

My heart thumped and I shivered as chill fingers of fear and anticipation ran up my spine. What kind of gift would a kelpie king give me?

Would it be something pretty, romantic, practical, magical—would it drive me insane?

I discovered early in life that touching unknown objects could lead to terrifying visions. I was nine years old when my psychic gift reared its ugly, traumatizing head. I've been wary of receiving gifts ever since.

Strong emotions leave behind an imprint. People like me, with a talent for psychometry, can tap into that psychic imprint and see glimpses of an object or persons' past.

Psychometry requires physical contact, thank Mab. That's the reason why I wear gloves twenty-four-seven. It's definitely not a fashion statement—Jinx is the fashionista in this friendship. I had learned the hard way that covering my hands helped to keep me sane.

Too bad an impermeable, full body suit wasn't practical. In fact, it would be potentially fatal. I may be part fae, but my human half still has to breathe. Plus, Jinx would never let me leave our loft apartment dressed in a full body condom. That would be breaking too many fashion rules. Alas, I should have been a pooka.

"Pfft," Jinx said with a shrug. "Ceffyl is king of the kelpies, give the guy a break. I'm sure he isn't thrilled to be swimming in the freezing cold ocean while negotiating boring hunting treaties between kelpie and selkie tribes."

It was true. Ceffyl hadn't been happy about cancelling our date. He'd broken a length of wooden railing in frustration when the call came in.

*****

We'd been walking along the waterfront under the stars, our new favorite pastime, when Ceff had stopped to stare intently at the bay. Ceff leaned casually against the railing, but I could hear his teeth grinding over the lapping sound of the waves.

A head surfaced near the docks, bobbing like a fishing buoy on the gentle waves of the harbor. The water fae waved its webbed hands and began speaking to Ceff in a high-pitched chatter that sounded similar to the squeaks and chirps of dolphin song. The words were unintelligible to my ears, but the message was clear. Ceff was needed elsewhere.

And when duty calls, kelpie kings have to listen. He wasn't happy about it. Storm clouds passed across Ceff's dark green eyes, making them shift to black, and he held the railing in a white-knuckled grip.

Ceff nodded once toward the bay and, with a strange bobbing bow, the water fae messenger returned to the dark waters from which he came. Ceff continued to stare into the harbor as if he could alter the message the tides had brought him by will alone. I held my breath and waited.

"I regret that I must cancel our date for tomorrow evening," Ceff said.

His voice sounded calm, like a gentle burbling stream, but the shattered railing beneath his hands told another story.

"But it's the tree lighting," I said. "It only happens once a year. Can't they wait one day?"

"I'm afraid not," he said. "My people and a neighboring selkie tribe are both insistent that if they do not gain exclusive fishing rights over one small patch of ocean, then they will starve to death. It is foolishness, and I suspect the truth behind the dispute will have little to do with food supplies, but I must go before a small argument spirals into a war between the water fae. It is my duty."

"Do you really think they'd wind up killing each other over a patch of water and some fish?" I asked.

"Fae wars have been started over much less," he said. "But do not worry. Selkies are some of the most peaceful of our kind. I am sure I can negotiate a treaty and return before the Winter Solstice."

"Okay," I said lamely. "At least we can still make it to Kaye's solstice celebration."

"Yes," he said. "Have you enquired about the dress code? Witches can be very particular about their festivals and ritual gatherings, especially the eight annual Sabbats."

Kaye had mentioned the dress code for her party alright. I felt my face burn.

"Clothing is optional," I said. I shook my head. "I'm going to need therapy after this party, but Kaye has done a lot to help me over the past few months. I can't turn down her invitation."

"Madam O'Shaye has done much for us all," he said.

True, Kaye did help to save the entire city of Harborsmouth. The least we could do was attend her holiday ritual.

"Well, don't get too excited about the dress code," I said. "I'm wearing clothing. Not really a big fan of public nudity, or hypothermia."

"I can think of ways to keep warm," he said. His eyes smoldered, shifting from black to bright luminous green.

I took an involuntary step back. Not at Ceff's otherness,
I actually thought his glowing eyes were sexy, but at the threat
of what they promised.

Ceff and I had been dating for a few months now, but we
hadn't actually touched yet. No hand holding or stolen kisses
in the dark. I had already experienced traumatic visions from
handling a piece of Ceff's bridle and wasn't quite ready to risk
touching the man himself. Coming into physical contact with
something old always increased the risk of multiple visions,
and Ceff was ancient. What would it be like to kiss an
immortal kelpie king?

I wasn't ready to find out, yet.

I dug in my pocket, covering my retreat by checking my
phone. No new messages. That in itself was a Christmas
miracle.

Ever since I agreed to take Forneus' first case, and
helped to protect the city against invading, bloodthirsty *each
uisge,* our phones had been ringing off the hook. Jinx had cases
scheduled for every day of the week going into the New Year.
Business at Private Eye investigations was booming.

Apparently, the fae who lived in Harborsmouth were in
need of a private investigator. Jinx and I were happy to fill
that niche. But working with fae meant calls at all hours, and
Jinx could only field so many of our clients.

More often than not, the job was something that
couldn't wait. When someone with fangs and claws shows up
and says it's urgent, you know it's a real emergency. Your
options are to either drop everything or turn tail and run. I
really picked the wrong time for a social life.

I guess I should give Ceff a break. I'd had to cancel my
share of dates due to emergency cases.

But now here we were, Ceff and I alone with no beasties
breathing down my neck for the services of Ivy Granger psychic
detective and Ceff had to leave.

Story of my life.

                              *****

Jinx rolled her eyes at me while I went back to sipping
my noxious coffee. I was at Jinx's mercy when it came to the
grocery shopping, since touching shopping carts and bags of
coffee beans was always a bad idea, so I tried to keep her in a

good mood. Maybe I could convince her to buy some real coffee. The kind that didn't taste like it was brewed with cookies, or someone's old fruit cake.

"Sorry, you're right," I said. "Ceff didn't really want to go. I'm just frustrated."

"Of course you're frustrated," Jinx said. She put a hand on one voluptuous hip and pointed a well-manicured finger at me. "You're a twenty-four-year-old virgin."

"Well...well, I have a unicorn!" I said.

I crossed my arms wishing Jinx would butt out of my non-existent sex life. I'd hoped that she'd back off once I started dating. Instead, my relationship with Ceff just seemed to fuel her need to interfere.

Jinx turned and wiped her eyes with a dish towel. Was she crying? I was grumpy, but Jinx was used to my mood swings, especially before my first cup of coffee. She set down the towel, looked at me, and started laughing.

"Oh my God, you should see yourself right now," she said.

"What?" I asked.

"Dude, you sound like you're five," she said. "And you're dressed in little kid pajamas."

"You bought me these pajamas," I said.

"I know," she said, sniffing and dabbing at her makeup.

"You suck," I said.

"Yes," she said.

"And this coffee tastes like stale cookies," I said.

"Totally," she said, nodding. "It was a Christmas gift from Olly. He has a skateboard competition in Oakland, so he dropped it off last night before leaving town."

"He bought us coffee?" I asked.

"He probably regifted it," she said, shrugging one tattooed shoulder.

"That makes more sense," I said. "And he's too much of a conspiracy buff to drink something someone else gave him. At least it wasn't Kool-Aid. He would have freaked."

"Plus, one whiff and he'd know it smelled like gingerbread men died in there," she said. "It's no wonder he gave the whole bag away."

"Seriously," I said. "Nastiest coffee ever."

"Want another cup?" she asked.

"Sure," I said.

It tasted gross, but a girl needs her caffeine fix. I gulped it down while Jinx took another dainty sip.

"You know what?" Jinx asked. "This probably tastes exactly like cookie monster pee."

I spit gingerbread coffee all over the counter. Jinx could be a total pain, but she really has a way with words.

And the two of us living together?—always entertaining.

CHAPTER 2

I was finishing up with my morning client when I heard a commotion at the front of the office. Greeting clients was Jinx's job, but with the variety of faeries seeking our services lately, I figured I'd better check things out.

There aren't any walls between my desk and Jinx's, or the front door, but the mother bugbear sitting in front of me was doing a fine impersonation. Adult bugbears are not only huge, but they're also covered in fur. This one's auburn fur stuck out in every direction, making it impossible to see what was happening at the front of the room.

I stood, on the pretense of fetching a glass of water, and peered around the bulk of my oversized client.

Damn. Forneus was standing in our office doorway and Jinx was brandishing a sharpened cross like she was a rockabilly incarnation of Buffy the vampire slayer. As I watched in horror, Jinx lifted the edge of her dress and slid a second cross from a sheath on her thigh. My office assistant got bonus points for style and preparedness, but I really didn't think killing our clients was good for business—especially with a bugbear sitting, oblivious, at my desk. Any second now my satisfied client was going to turn around and reconsider the agency she hired, and our payment.

No way was I losing that fee. Tracking down that cub took me over a week. And bugbear wrangling is no treat. I worked hard for every penny and I wasn't letting Jinx and Forneus' flirtatious fighting scare off my client.

Plus, I needed that money to pay for coffee. There was no way I was beginning another day drinking the stuff Olly gifted us. Not after Jinx's comment. I'd picture a fuzzy, blue monster singing "C is for coffee" while peeing into my cup.

That settled it. I needed to take control of the situation, quickly.

"Let me just get the invoice from my assistant and we'll be done here," I said, smiling at the bugbear.

I tried not to show my teeth. Flash too much tooth and some predators will think you are issuing a challenge. I did not need to add a bugbear pissing contest to an already bad situation. I don't think our office would survive that level of chaos. I know that I'm not up for that fight. Have you seen the size of their claws?

I walked casually past the bugbear who was eyeing my dish of honey candies. I discovered while hanging out with my friends Marvin and Hob, a bridge troll and a brownie, that pureblood fae have a weakness for sweets, especially honey. I kept the dish of candies on hand for situations like these.

Now that my clientele has changed, I may not be able to keep the office warded and filled with anti-fae charms, but I still kept a few tricks up my sleeve. It never hurt to be prepared.

"What do you two think you're doing?" I hissed. I turned my full wrath on Jinx. She didn't even flinch. Guess I can't be scary when a person's seen me in my snowman pajamas. "What happened?"

"That damn demon is here again," Jinx said, never taking her eyes off Forneus. "That's what happened."

"That's all?" I asked. "He came through the door and you tried to stake him with a cross?"

"I can assure you that I have done nothing untoward," Forneus said. His sulphuric breath made me gag. "I merely offered this lovely lady a compliment."

"What did he call you this time?" I asked.

"He called me his pet," she said through clenched teeth. "I warned him last time that if he addressed me that way again, I'd kill him."

"She did warn you," I said, turning to the demon. I took a step forward to stand between them. "But, as much as I'd like to see her cut you with that cross, I have a client waiting—a *paying* client."

That last bit of info was for Jinx. She immediately lowered her weapons and slid them neatly into her hair and up the skirt of her halter dress.

"I'll get the paperwork," Jinx said. She hurried to her desk and pointed at the chairs arranged beside it. "You take a seat, demon. And don't even think about leaving one of your business cards in my waiting room."

"Yes, ma'am," he said.

The demon folded himself primly into one of our mismatched chairs—mismatched because we had to douse a chair with holy water and trash it after one of Forneus' earlier visits. Just for the record, burning brimstone is Hell on upholstery. He was lucky we let him walk through our doors at all.

I walked back to mother bugbear, who was miraculously still sitting facing my desk. A glance at my empty candy dish showed why. I'd have to restock my supply soon.

I saw a trip to the candy store in my future.

I may not like to shop, but going to the candy store with Marvin was a treat. I didn't have to touch anything, since the kid was happy to put everything in the basket for me. With no worries about psychic visions, I could kick back and watch Marvin's smile grow.

Marvin's smile was worth the effort. His mouth was healing from his previous injuries and the kid was looking better by the day. Not that anyone in the candy shop could see his true face. Marvin was one of the fae, a teenage bridge troll, and wore his glamour whenever we hit the streets.

I'd check in with Marvin later. I had an errand to run at Madam Kaye's Magic Emporium, and Hob was still allowing Marvin to sleep on the floor of the spell kitchen, out behind the shop. The place may be owned by Kaye O'Shaye, the most powerful witch in Harborsmouth, but Hob, the resident hearth brownie, was in charge of the kitchen. I could visit Marvin, get the items I needed from The Emporium, and be back before dark...if Forneus didn't hold me up.

"Here you are," Jinx said, setting a folder on my desk. Jinx beamed at the bugbear as she pointed to the folder. "Just read and sign the last page. And make checks payable to Private Eye. We're also happy to accept cash and all major credit cards."

The mother bugbear lifted a leather pouch onto the desk with a thud. Gold coins spilled from the bag as she scratched her mark onto the page, with her claws.

"Ivy?" Jinx asked.

I knew what Jinx was asking. In addition to psychometry, I also have the gift of second sight. My second sight allows me to see through the glamour that most fae wear to the monstrous visage that lies beneath. This was another gift that could feel like a curse, but it was a talent that came in handy when accepting payment from faeries.

Fae, both Seelie and Unseelie, have an aversion to paying humans real money. Since humans usually can't see through magical glamour, faeries often pay with illusionary money that reverts to its original worthless form after they have safely gone. It wouldn't be the first time that a faerie tried to pay with leaves and twigs. But this gold was real.

And I wasn't human.

I nodded to Jinx.

"We also accept gold," Jinx said, smiling.

Jinx led the bugbear out the door and I strode over to where Forneus sat in his expensive suit. I crossed my arms and tapped my foot.

"Okay, demon, why are you here?" I asked.

Forneus spread his hands and opened his eyes wide in mock surprise.

"Can't a friend drop in without a reason?" he asked. "'Tis the season after all. Perhaps I'm here to spread holiday cheer."

"Or an STD," Jinx muttered.

Jinx closed the door behind our bugbear client and came to sit on the edge of her desk. She sucked air through her teeth and winced. The reason became clear when she pulled a thumb tack from her generous derriere. Jinx really was the most unlucky person on the planet. Which made taunting a demon a ridiculously bad idea.

"I will have you know that..." Forneus said.

"No," I said, holding up a gloved hand. "No way. I do not want to hear about your sexual exploits. I don't care where your pitchfork has been, Forneus, just keep it in your pants."

"Amen," Jinx said.

Forneus grimaced at the holy word, but continued to leer at Jinx. She was adjusting the bust of her fifties-style halter dress in a not so subtle attempt to drive Forneus crazy. Watching the demon lust over my best friend made my stomach heave. It was time to change the subject.

"So what's the job?" I asked, rubbing my brow. Forneus had only been here a few minutes and already I had a headache. "And don't tell me that this is just a social call."

"Well, I do have information you may find valuable," Forneus said. "For a price."

Forneus' eyes glowed red and his face shifted as the muscles writhed beneath the skin. It was a reminder that our guest wasn't human. Forneus may wear a handsome face while doing business, but his preferred form while topside was a leviathan-like beast the size of our entire city block. I didn't know what form the demon attorney took when residing in Hell, but the glowing red eyes were a clue.

I stifled a shudder and met those eyes determined not to let Forneus get the upper hand.

"No deals with the devil, Forneus," I said. "If your information is useful, we can work something out, but no souls, or dates with my partner, as payment. And if what you have to say isn't of use to us, then we owe you nothing."

Forneus steepled his fingers and frowned, deep in thought. After three minutes, I was beginning to wonder if he'd fallen asleep. Do demons sleep? I'd have to ask Father Michael the next time I went to visit Galliel at Sacred Heart church.

"If this becomes a significant case, I want full credit for bringing this information to you," he said.

Demons were always fighting to advance within their social hierarchy and Forneus was no different. He had received a promotion for his role in bringing me the kelpie case, and the resulting battle that case had caused. Now I couldn't get rid of the ambitious fiend.

"Deal," I said.

The demon reached a hand out to shake on our agreement, and I danced out of reach.

"You know the rules," I said, voice hardening.

"Ah, yes," he said, leaning back in his chair. "No touching."

"So we have a deal?" I asked.

"Deal," he said.

A grin spread over his face and I began to doubt my decision to agree so quickly.

"What did you find out?" I asked.

"Someone is killing fae, right here in Harborsmouth," he said.

I really was going to regret this. Forneus wasn't bringing me a typical lost and found case, he was talking about murder.

"How many dead?" I asked.

"Five that I know of, all fae," he said. "And before you ask, they are not all Seelie or Unseelie. Both courts have received victims."

Oh, Oberon's eyes. If the victims had all been from one court, then I'd know where to begin looking for their killer. But this wasn't an overzealous faerie trying to curry favor with their Lord by assassinating members of the opposing court. This was something else entirely.

There was a serial killer in Harborsmouth with a penchant for murdering faeries. Happy freaking holidays.

CHAPTER 3

According to Forneus, five fae had been murdered on the streets of Harborsmouth. But what did a peri, a hamadryad, a merry dancer, a pixie, and old Fear Dearg have in common?

The only clue to tie these deaths together was a piece of mistletoe left at each scene. Well, that and the fact that shortly after each victim was discovered, their body disappeared.

Since mistletoe was our one clue, Christmas was the obvious connection. Maybe someone had a thing against Santa's elves and was killing the next best thing.

I shook my head. No, that was just silly. Santa didn't exist and the elves had left our shores long ago.

But why kill these particular fae?

I stared at the list I'd hastily penciled onto a notepad, trying to make sense of these murders. If I couldn't ferret out the truth on my own, I'd have to ask Kaye for help. And if I couldn't find answers at The Emporium, I'd have to visit each of the crime scenes. Touching a person's wedding ring to see if they've been cheating on their spouse is one thing, but handling items at a murder scene is quite another. I shuddered and returned my focus to the notepad on my desk.

Peris are small, winged men often mistaken for angels. Their diminutive size makes them vulnerable to their natural enemy, the daeva, who enjoy locking them in iron cages at the tops of trees. Had our killer wanted a sick tree topper for his Christmas tree?

I shook my head, trying to shake away the image. I was just letting the holidays, and my own dark mood, get to me, right? Maybe the other victims would reveal a pattern.

A hamadryad was the second faerie on the list. Hamadryads are tree nymphs who are peaceful unless their tree is threatened. Hamadryads are very protective of their chosen tree and have been known to keep a tree alive for hundreds of years. But if a hamadryad dies, the tree they are bound to die with it. Forneus indicated that this hamadryad had come from a fir tree, which was peculiar for a city dryad. There aren't many trees in Harborsmouth and even fewer evergreens. I wonder which city park or old tree lined street was mourning the loss of its fir tree. Or had the killer cut it down as a gruesome souvenir?

This case was beginning to leave a bad taste in my mouth worse than this morning's coffee.

I didn't know a lot about my cousins the merry dancers. While researching my wisp heritage, I'd found mention of them, but most sources just referenced the beautiful, colorful lights they produced when they danced through the air. Do merry dancers continue to glow after death? Had the merry dancer been killed to light the hamadryad's tree?

I glared at the list of victims, gripping my pencil so hard the edges bit through my thick gloves. A tree, an angel, and lights? Mab's bloody bones, holidays were Hell.

I wasn't surprised to see a pixie on the list of victims. Even I'd been tempted to kill a few of the pests over the years. Pixies are the fae equivalent of wasps. They may have beautiful, iridescent wings, but don't let that fool you. The evil little creatures are armed with a stinger the size of a hypodermic needle. One sting will paralyze a grown human, but pixies are rarely solitary. As soon as one of the bastards has you down, the entire hive is likely to use your body as a salt lick. Pixies survive on salt, too bad their saliva is an allergen that itches like the devil. Take it from me; being pixed sucks.

Was the pixie now hanging as a bloody ornament on the killer's tree, iridescent wings reflecting a rainbow of color in the glow of the merry dancer's light? The thought made bile rise in my throat. I may not like the little insects, but no one deserved to be strung on a tree. Not even a pixie.

Fear Dearg was the one faerie on the list whom I had met. I had made the mistake of running errands during the holidays last year and got turned around. As the maze-like store became more crowded, a band of iron tightened around my chest. I needed to escape the press of shoppers before I hyperventilated and passed out. I did not want to be one of those holiday victims trampled to death by their fellow shoppers.

I was ready to vault onto a display case and take my chances running along the tops of shopping carts and clothing racks when Fear Dearg had appeared. Dressed in a red coat and hat and long white beard, he looked like a stand-in for old Saint Nick. He had pointed to the exit, put a finger to his nose, and vanished. When I mentioned the encounter later, Kaye told me that Fear Dearg had once been a benevolent faerie who helped lost travelers on the moors. But the moors and peat bogs had been drained. Now Fear Dearg helped Allmart shoppers find their way to the housewares department, and lead panicky psychics to the exit. The modern world hadn't been kind to some of the fae. And now someone had killed the poor man.

"Are we really taking this case?" Jinx asked.

I thought about old Fear Dearg's rosy-cheeked smile as he helped me find my way out of that store filled with holiday shoppers.

"Yes," I said. "I think this sicko is killing fae to create some kind of twisted Christmas diorama."

Jinx wrinkled her nose.

"Sounds like a total nut job," Jinx said. "Leave it to the holidays to bring out the crazies."

Jinx was right. The holidays are dangerous enough when the people going insane are human. Add faeries, demons, and the undead to the mix and you get a recipe for something truly nasty. Now we just had to figure out who was doing the killing.

And who was stealing the bodies.

I swallowed hard and reached for the cup of water I'd left sitting beside the dish of honey candies. We had our water cooler blessed by a local priest, but the holy water didn't taste any different than regular spring water. Holy water doesn't have any effect on faeries, but throw it on a demon and you had a weapon more corrosive than hydrochloric acid. Too bad we weren't dealing with a demon. That much seemed obvious.

A demon wouldn't have left sprigs of mistletoe floating in a pool of blood. Demons reap souls, preferring to play with their prey in Hell where they are at their most powerful. If our killer was a demon, he'd have left only a charred, soulless husk behind.

"I don't think our nut job is a demon," I said.

Jinx snorted. "Why not?" she asked.

Jinx rested her hand on her skirt where I'd seen one of her sharpened crosses disappear. I was glad we weren't looking for Hellspawn. I'd never keep Jinx safely in the office if we were gunning for a demon. Forneus had a habit of getting under her skin and today's visit hadn't helped her aversion toward demons.

"Nothing was burned at the scene," I said, tapping the notepad. "No charred remains."

"Okay, gag, that's nasty," she said. "But shouldn't we check the crime scenes ourselves? I don't trust Forneus. It would be just like that creep to leave out an important detail like faeries fried extra crispy or a lingering cloud of sulphur and brimstone."

Sadly, Jinx was right. I couldn't trust Forneus. I'd have to see the crime scenes for myself.

"I'll check the scenes later," I said. "But first I need to ask Kaye about the victims. She has more knowledge of the supernatural races than anyone else in the city. If there's a connection I'm missing, she'll know."

"Ask her to check with her Hunter friends too," she said. "Maybe they've heard something about the murders. And, of course, if they want to lend one of their big, strong, Hunters to come protect our offices, I won't complain."

Jinx batted her eyelashes and tried to look helpless. I knew better. She may look like a rockabilly damsel in distress, but Jinx could flay a person's soul with a good tongue lashing. She could give a drill sergeant a run for his money. I should know. She spent most of her time keeping me in line.

"I'd ask, but they'd probably send Jenna," I said.

Jenna was a young, female Hunter I'd met during the *each uisge* invasion of Harborsmouth. Jenna is petite, wears her flame red hair in a short, cute, pixie cut, and is always armed to the teeth. When we first met she wore a sword at her hip, knives in a forearm sheath, a gun holster strapped around her thigh, and held a crossbow trained at my head. I have that effect on people.

"I need some eye candy," Jinx said waggling her eyebrows. "Tell them to send Hans."

Hans was a tall, Nordic drink of water who looked like a Norse God. Fought like one too. The guy was gorgeous enough to give Jinx a toothache, but Hans was also known for his berserker-like rages. Angry rampaging on the battlefield was usually beneficial, especially when the desired outcome was a high body count, but it wasn't a quality I wanted in someone dating my best friend. Leave it to Jinx to always pick the bad boys.

"Sure, I'll do that," I said, rolling my eyes. "While I'm at it, I'll ask a leprechaun for his pot of gold. I have about the same chances of him saying yes."

The Hunter's Guild didn't owe me any favors. In fact, their assistance in the recent battle against the *each uisge* army had helped to save my city. I knew that the Hunters hadn't fought for me, they were there to back up Kaye, a former hunter, and to defend the humans of Harborsmouth, but it felt like I owed them. Of course, if they ever wanted to collect on that debt, they'd have to get in line.

"Then bring me back a coffee," she said, pouting. "That demon gave me a headache."

"That, I can do," I said.

I pulled on my coat, tucking the notepad in one pocket and a fistful of charms into another. Being half-fae had its perks. Most anti-fae charms, such as rowanberry, stale bread, clothing turned inside out, four-leafed clovers, and cold iron, didn't affect me.

We may have put away most of our protection items in consideration for our new clientele, but that didn't mean I went around unarmed. I kept a stash of iron nails, sharpened stakes, holy water, and silver crosses in my desk drawer. I was an equal opportunity kind of girl—you never know what might slink, slither, crawl, fly, or dance through your door. It was best to be prepared for the worst.

If a faerie, a vampire, and a demon walk into a bar, you wait for the punch line. At Private Eye, when a faerie, a vampire, and a demon walk through the door, it's just another day at the office.

CHAPTER 4

If it wasn't for the holidays, winter would be my favorite season. A cold, arctic wind blew across the harbor to tug at my scarf and bite my nose. I pulled my coat tighter and smiled.

Winter is the one time of year when I feel normal. I can walk the streets of Harborsmouth without strange looks, curious stares, and stolen glances. Wearing gloves when it's freezing cold outside is completely reasonable, but wear those same gloves in the melting heat of summer and passerby are likely to think you belong locked away with Aunt Edna's fruitcake.

I ignored the wreath and garland-bedecked lamp posts as I made my way through the Old Port toward Kaye's shop. Holiday decorations?—bah humbug. I'd rather the city invest its money in putting sand on our sidewalks.

I trudged through the slush along the curb, avoiding the ice slick walkways. The sidewalks in this part of town were made of dark red brick that matched the old buildings that lined the street. During the day, water dripped down from icicles the size of yeti fangs to threaten those who walked beneath and dampen the ice below. At night the puddles froze, turning this brick sidewalk into a narrow skating rink...at a forty-five degree pitch. More than one drunk had stumbled out the door of an Old Port bar and ended up in the harbor.

I'd take my chances with the cobblestone street.

I turned up Wharf Street where Madame Kaye's Magic Emporium perched at the top of the hill like a queen in a purple and midnight blue gown trimmed with gold. Astrological symbols covered the wood and brick façade while overflowing cauldrons, tarot decks, Halloween costumes, and packets of herbs fought for space in the shop windows.

I hurried my pace, the wind now at my back, and pushed open the door. Wind chimes sang and the plastic bones of skeletons rattled as a rush of cold air made its way into the store.

"Close the door, dear, before my face freezes this way," Kaye said.

I pushed the door closed and turned to see Kaye glaring at her assistant Arachne with one eye scrunched up tight. Arachne was facing Kaye and mirroring the expression.

"Um, am I interrupting something?" I asked.

Kaye was the most powerful witch in all of Harborsmouth, possibly the entire eastern seaboard. If she was angry, I wanted to be somewhere else, fast.

"Hey, Ivy," Arachne said. She smiled and waved, the angry expression leaving her face. "Kaye was teaching me the Evil Eye. Cool, huh?"

Arachne worked part time at The Emporium in hopes of becoming Kaye's apprentice. Arachne was sixteen, blond, and a hard worker. She was also completely gullible.

Kaye likes to play tricks on her human employees, which is why they usually don't last long. Arachne had been here the longest, but Kaye never tired of pranking her. If I didn't know better, I'd say Kaye had a puck in her bloodline.

I looked over at Kaye, who was pulling faces behind Arachne's back, and groaned.

"Are you going to tell her, or should I?" I asked.

Kaye started laughing, the bells on her bracelets and anklets jingling, and waved for me to go on. I turned back to Arachne and her face fell.

"Oh, it wasn't a real lesson, was it?" she asked.

"Sorry, kid," I said.

Kaye let out a snort and dabbed at her kohl-rimmed eyes with the corner of her head scarf.

"Don't worry, dear," Kaye said. "I'll teach you a truth spell later. It will be worth more to you than an Evil Eye."

It was true that Arachne could use a truth spell working here, but knowing Kaye she'd know a way around her own spell. It wouldn't do to spoil her fun and trickery.

Arachne nodded and moved behind the counter where she started counting and tagging packets of incense. Kaye hustled toward the rear of the store and I followed. The jumble of wares that cluttered the aisles closed around us as we made our way to the back of the store where a secret button let us past the counter, through a beaded curtain, and into a hallway that led to Kaye's small office on one side and her spell kitchen on the other.

Kaye turned left and I followed her into the kitchen where Marvin sat on the floor. Hob was flitting around Marvin's head, attaching something to his face.

"Hello, Hob," I said. I acknowledged Hob first, since brownies were particular about such things, and easily angered. Orphaned bridge trolls, on the other hand, were much more forgiving. "Hello, Marvin."

"Hello, Poison Ivy," Marvin said, grinning.

The kid never got tired of that one. Hob fussed as the gray stuff he was attaching to Marvin's face shifted with the wide grin. Hob harrumphed and stomped a booted foot on Marvin's shoulder.

"Told ye ta sit still," Hob said.

"Why don't you both take a break," Kaye said.

I thought Hob would complain, but instead, he flew toward me so fast I stumbled over my own two feet. He stopped, perching on a pot hook above my head. There was a greedy gleam in the eyes that peeked from below his large, bushy brow.

"Where be me gift?" Hob asked.

I may have a fear of handling strange gifts, but Hob had no such compunction. I had entered the hearth brownie's domain and he expected his payment. It was tradition and faeries take such things very seriously indeed.

I dipped my gloved hand into the pocket of my coat and pulled out a small pigeon feather wrapped in shiny tissue paper. I always kept small gifts with me in case I visited Kaye's kitchen. I'd rather stumble into a nest of pixies than enter Hob's domain without bringing his payment. There is nothing worse than an angry brownie.

I set the present on the nearby counter and stepped away. Hob circled the tiny package, dancing a jig on the white tiled countertop. Even if he didn't care for the dove gray feather, I figured he'd like the tissue paper. Brownies adore shiny things.

Hob pounced on the package, stripping the tissue from the feather. He examined the feather so closely it tickled his bulbous red nose. His nose twitched, but Hob continued to hold the feather to his face.

"Is the gift acceptable?" I asked.

As much as I enjoyed visiting with Hob and Marvin, I really did have questions for Kaye. My father's blood may add extra years to my lifespan, but I couldn't wait around here forever. Whoever was killing faeries in our city had to be stopped.

"Aye, lass," Hob said.

I let out the breath I'd been holding and moved further into the kitchen.

"So what's with the getup?" I asked, nodding at Marvin.

"Play," Marvin said.

Were the troll and brownie playing dress up? That was new.

"We are putting on a theatrical performance," Kaye said. "During the solstice party."

"Aye, the Changeling Child," Hob said. He put a knobby finger to the side of his nose.

"I don't think I've seen that one," I said. "What part are you playing, Marvin?"

"Wise man," he said.

Now that I thought about it, the cloth covering Marvin's head and shoulders did resemble a hooded cloak. The gray stuff Hob had been attaching to Marvin's face must have been a beard.

"And you, Hob?" I asked.

"Ta changeling babe!" he said, slapping his knee. Hob laughed and wiped his eyes with the back of his sleeve. "Dis wise man bring me gold."

I had a sinking feeling about what holiday story they were doing a faerie retelling of. The image of the shriveled old brownie swaddled in a manger made me cringe. Changeling tales had always given me the creeps.

Faeries rarely have children of their own and have been known to steal human infants. The human child is whisked away and an elderly faerie left in its place. The unsuspecting humans will often take care of the invalid fae while their baby is raised by faeries. Unfortunately, faerie child rearing often includes slave-like servitude. I hid my shudder with a shrug.

"Cool, can't wait to see the show," I said. "So, Kaye, I had an interesting visitor today."

"Was it that demon?" she asked.

"Yes," I said, tilting my head to the side. "How did you know?"

"I strengthened my wards," she said. Kaye had been upset when Forneus first entered the city without her knowledge. Apparently, she'd been working to remedy that problem. "An alarm sounds when a demon enters the city, but he was gone before I had a chance to investigate."

"Is that the only demon you've sensed entering Harborsmouth recently?" I asked.

"Yes, no other demon would be so foolish," she said.

That confirmed my original suspicion. Our killer wasn't a demon. We were looking for a faerie, an undead, or…a human.

I filled Kaye, Marvin, and Hob in on the details of the case. Kaye stomped across the floor, jewelry jingling and skirts rustling as she paced back and forth. She may be a retired Hunter, but Kaye was a fierce protector of this city. Knowing that someone had managed to kill five fae under her nose had upset her.

Marvin chewed his lip and stared at the floor.

Hearing about faerie murders had to be hard on the kid. A bridge troll probably doesn't sound like an easy target for a beating, but Marvin was a teenager and an orphan. He had been struggling to live alone on the streets when the *each uisge* came to Harborsmouth. When the bloodthirsty water fae attacked, the kid never stood a chance. If the *each uisge* hadn't had more interesting prey that night, Marvin would be dead. His wounds were healing, but the emotional scars were going to take a while longer.

Good thing I knew a way to cheer the kid up.

"Hey, Marvin," I said. "My bugbear client ate all of the honey candies in my office. Want to take a trip to the candy store later?"

Marvin nodded and smiled.

"How about you take off your costume, dear, while I speak to Ivy in my office," Kaye said.

Kaye bustled out into the hallway and I hurried to catch up.

"I'll be back in an hour, Marvin," I said, following Kaye to the door. "Hour and a half tops. I have a few items to stock up on from the shop and then I'll come meet you here." I waved to both Marvin and Hob. "Safe travels."

"Safe travels, lass," Hob said.

I entered Kaye's office to a cloud of dust that made my eyes water. I pinched my nose, stifling a sneeze, and watched as Kaye used her magic to move books and documents around the room. Books covered every surface of Kaye's office and formed precarious towers that reached to the ceiling. With a twitch of Kaye's finger and a twist of her wrist, leather bound tomes and yellowed papers slid out of the leaning towers and whizzed past her face. If it wasn't for Kaye's magic, we'd be buried in a book avalanche.

"Here it is," Kaye said, holding an object triumphantly over her head.

I moved closer, ducking as a sheaf of papers flew past my nose. I stepped back, not wanting anything of Kaye's to touch my bare skin. Kaye may be my friend, but her arcane collection of spell tomes, ritual items, and occult books has been passed down from one magic user to the next—steeped in centuries of blood and madness.

The papers rustled as they rushed forward and slid beneath one of the book towers to my left. I held my breath as a crystal ball, which had been sitting atop the stack of books, teetered back and forth. If the scrying crystal tipped over the edge, I knew one private investigator who wouldn't be catching it.

Kaye reached up to smooth her wild raven locks, and I let out a sigh of relief as the items settled back into place. She waved me forward and I tiptoed through piles of magical detritus as if compelled. But this time Kaye wasn't using her magic. My boots were finding their way across the office because of the item in Kaye's hand. Her heavily beringed fingers held a well-worn volume from a set of herbal encyclopedias.

Of course, Kaye's compendium of herbs went beyond what plants to grow in your garden. These books contained the magical uses, both good and wicked, for each herb—seed, stem, leaf, and root. I had perused a few of these volumes when researching protection charms. Some of the entries were fairly benign, but others had left my stomach in knots and had given me nightmares for a week. Since I already had my share of nightmares, I hoped the information on mistletoe fell into the safe and boring category.

No such luck.

"Here," Kaye said.

With another puff of dust, Kaye dropped the open book onto her desk and tapped the page with one tattooed finger. The black swirls of ink hadn't reached her hands before the *each uisge* attack. I winced and made a mental note to ask her about it later. It seemed like lately, all I had for my friend was questions.

I leaned forward to see what Kaye was pointing at. The old etching depicted a man reaching for his throat. His eyes were bulging and his tongue was black.

Mistletoe was poisonous. It was also used during the holidays as an excuse to sneak a kiss. I wasn't sure which was worse.

According to the book, mistletoe was poisonous when the leaves or berries were ingested. It was also considered dangerous to inhale the smoke. For these reasons, mistletoe was not used in magical teas, tisanes, incense, and ritual fires. However, the plant did have many magical uses.

Mistletoe was used by the Druids to alter states of consciousness and induce visions. The plant was also commonly used in ritual sacrifice. I swallowed hard and skimmed past the diagrams depicting the stomach contents of sacrificial victims.

My leather glove creaked like a coffin lid as I rubbed at the back of my stooped neck. Could our killer be reenacting some form of ritualistic murder? I sure hope not. Reading one encyclopedic entry on sacrifice was enough nightmare fodder for an entire lifetime.

In the cases of sacrifice involving mistletoe, the victims were force fed the plant then subjected to a three-fold death. The first death was caused by blows to the head with a blunt instrument. The second death involved strangulation, hanging, or breaking of the neck. The third death was secured with a blade to the victim's carotid artery. Got to love that human sacrifice.

"This three-fold death thing is disgusting," I said.

I pointed to the sketch of a victim succumbing to each stage of death. The drawing was worse than the diagram of stomach contents.

"The number three is significant to humans and the fae," Kaye said, shrugging. "At least the victims ate or imbibed the mistletoe first. That was a kindness. The sacrificial lamb would hallucinate and die from poison before realizing the horrors of the first beating."

Kaye seemed unfazed by the stories of sacrifice. Had she taken part in such a ritual in her past? I shook my head. No way. My friend may have a practical approach to magic and its uses, but she wouldn't step over that line. Kaye had given her life to protecting humans. She wouldn't go around using them as spell components.

"So mistletoe is a poison and a part of murderous rituals," I said. "What else?"

I had a feeling that Kaye knew most of the wisdom found in her library.

"Mistletoe is a magical amplifier," Kaye said. "Adding the plant or berries to almost any magic, good or evil, will increase the desired outcome of a spell. The mistletoe that grows on oak trees is the most powerful, but any type will do."

"Great, this stuff acts like a shot of energy drink to casters," I said. "Is that it?"

"Just a question, dear," she said. "Was there anything else at the scene? Perhaps something that could indicate what magic, if any, was being used."

I thought back to my conversation with Forneus. According to the demon, the only thing left at the crime scenes, once the bodies disappear, was mistletoe and blood. I ran a gloved hand through my hair and voiced the idea that came unbidden to my lips.

"Blood," I said. "At every scene there was blood. I assumed it was from the act of murder itself. But..."

"It could be something else entirely," she said, nodding. "Blood magic is powerful, hostile. Mistletoe may amplify the outcome of a spell, but blood amplifies both the magic and the emotions of the caster."

"Let me guess," I said, giving Kaye a mirthless smile. "That doesn't usually end well."

"No, it never does," Kaye said. "Blood magic ends badly, indeed."

"Could someone be using this kind of magic in Harborsmouth without you knowing?" I asked, staring at the books that lined the walls.

I couldn't meet Kaye's eyes. She worked hard to spread her awareness over our city, like a magical security blanket to protect innocent humans from harm. But like any hand knit afghan, Kaye's awareness spell had holes. She had tightened the magical threads that detected demons, but that didn't mean something else couldn't slip through.

I darted my gaze in time to see my friend's shoulders slump. Kaye's head dipped to her chest as she let out a sigh. Kaye was a tough old bird. That sigh said it all.

"I'm not getting any younger, dear," Kaye said. She lifted her head to meet my eyes, but a bleak look had replaced the fire I was used to seeing reflected in their black depths. Kaye raised a hand, wiggling her fingers. The bell sleeves of her blouse fell back to reveal a mass of twining tattoos. "My magic comes at a price. I do what I can, but yes, someone could be practicing blood magic without my knowing."

Since the *each uisge* attack, I'd been lucky. Business was booming and Jinx and I had settled into our daily routine. I was courting an immortal kelpie king, and my witch friend, with the aid of every magic user in the region, had cast a spell more powerful than anything I'd ever seen. For the first time since becoming aware of the monsters that walked our streets, I had felt safe.

I was a fool.

Now I was taking another job from a demon, Ceffyl was away negotiating water fae treaties, someone was killing faeries like they were mosquitoes, and my all-powerful witch friend was admitting that she wasn't all-powerful after all. I ducked my head, feeling vulnerable. I felt like someone had attached a bull's eye to my back—right next to the "kick me" sign and "world's biggest idiot" post-it note. For most people, letting their guard down is a healthy thing. In Harborsmouth, it will just get you dead.

"Okay, what can I do?" I asked.

"Visit the murder scenes and see what else you can find," she said. "The sooner we know what we're dealing with,

the better. And Ivy? Don't forget your plan to stock up on
protection herbs and amulets. I'll call the front desk and
inform Arachne that you aren't to be charged for today's
purchases."

"Um, thanks," I said.

"Yes, of course, dear," she said, waving me away. "Now
go. After my call to Arachne, I will contact the Hunter's guild.
They should be made aware of the threat to the city. Hunters
may have vowed to protect humans against supernatural
forces, but they won't take kindly to someone murdering fae
without their permission."

"Are you sure a Hunter didn't make these kills?" I
asked.

"There have been no sanctioned kills or banishments in
over two weeks," she said. I raised an eyebrow and she sighed.
"I may be retired from active duty, but I retain an honorary
seat on the Hunter's council. They keep me apprised of guild
activities within Harborsmouth. Now go."

Kaye pulled a phone from her multi-layered skirts,
effectively ending our conversation. I hadn't known about
Kaye's involvement with the Hunter's council. My gaze darted
to the tattoos covering the hand holding the phone to her ear.
In fact, there was a lot I didn't know about my friend. But now,
as always, wasn't the time to ask.

I spun on my heel and left the room.

CHAPTER 5

The Emporium was nearly as cluttered as Kaye's office. The only place in the building that wasn't full of stuff preparing to topple over and smother me to death was Kaye's spell kitchen. That was because A) Hob would never tolerate a mess near his hearth and B) One speck of the wrong ingredient in Kaye's pot would spell KABOOM. The shop, however, belonged on an episode of Hoarders.

Plastic skeletons and foam reaper scythes battled for space alongside straw brooms, and faux spider webs. At least, I think the webs aren't real. I ducked lower, avoiding a basketball-sized spider with its plethora of beady eyes. That thing had to be fake, right? I sighed and shook web from my hair. You never can tell at The Emporium.

I dodged pointy hats, Styrofoam gargoyles, and overflowing cauldrons. Unlike the spell pots in Kaye's kitchen, these cauldrons were made of black plastic. Prettily labeled packets of herbs, mostly benign, spilled over the rim of each cauldron and onto tables and shelves.

I dipped the fingertips of one gloved hand gingerly into a nearby pot and withdrew small packages of wolfsbane, hellebore, mandrake, and agrimony. Most of the herbs at Madame Kaye's Magic Emporium were mundane, not all. These plants, and the salt in my pocket, would provide some protection against black magic. The rowanberry, stale bread, nails, and iron shavings I'd brought from my office stash would be my backup against faeries.

I grabbed a handful of glitter-topped wooden pencils from where they protruded from a grinning skull. Those were for any vamps that got in my way. Who said stakes can't be pretty?

I carried the goods to the front counter where Arachne hunched over a box of rubber bats, pricing gun at the ready.

"Hey," I said, setting the items on the countertop. "Kaye said these were on the house. Do you still want to ring them up?"

"Thanks, Ivy," Arachne said. "Keeping inventory around here is like trying to count grains of sand in an hourglass. Just give me a sec."

"Sure thing," I said.

"Need a bag?" she asked after ringing up the goods. Arachne held up a paper bag with the store logo across the front.

"No thanks," I said.

I scooped up the herbs and dumped them into the inner pocket of my coat. I tucked the pencils into the back of my belt, careful to keep my shirt between the wood and my skin. Most of my visions came from touching items with my hands, but that didn't mean the rest of my hide was safe.

"You heading back to the kitchen?" she asked.

"Just long enough to tell Marvin I have to bail on our candy run," I said. I sighed, not looking forward to that conversation. "Later, Arachne."

"Safe travels," she said.

I shambled back to the rear of the store, not eager to disappoint Marvin. The bridge troll was one of the few people who I cared about in this town. Oh well, nothing I could do about it now. Kaye had pressed the issue of time, which meant I couldn't be wandering off to the candy store with Marvin. Not today.

I needed to visit the crime scenes and see if there was any evidence of blood magic. Maybe knock on doors and find out if there were any fae witnesses to the attacks. That kind of legwork might be safe enough if I was looking for a lost necklace or a runaway bugbear, but this time I was searching for a stone cold killer. There was no way I'd risk taking the kid with me.

It was the right decision, but that didn't stop the guilt that gnawed away at my insides. I pressed the button that unlocked the rear counter and pushed through the bead curtain into the hallway at the back. With a sigh, I knocked on the kitchen door and stepped inside.

I hoped that Hob wouldn't want another gift, this soon after my last visit, but if he required it, I'd give him one of the pencils in my belt. The pencils were as long as his stumpy legs, but at least they were shiny.

"Hi Hob," I said, looking around the kitchen. "Where's Marvin?"

Hob was dusting the large mantel that hung about the hearth. The wood shone, but Hob rubbed at the mantel like it was covered in grime.

"Up n' disappeared!" he said. Hob continued to rub at the wood, but moisture shone in his eyes. "I only ducked inta me hole for a second. I swear eet. But when I returned, da wee mite was gone."

A pile of cloth and fur sat on the floor, the costume Marvin had changed out of. The kid wouldn't just leave a mess like that on Hob's floor. He was smarter than that. My heart sank and a chill entered the hollow pit of my stomach. I stared at the discarded clothing and let the importance of Hob's words sink in. A serial killer who was targeting fae was out there somewhere and now Marvin was missing. My hands tightened into fists, making the leather of my gloves creak.

"Don't worry," I said. "I'll find him. But Hob? Make sure Kaye knows about this and have her call me the second anyone learns anything."

"Find 'im, lass," he said.

Hob didn't look away from his polishing as I spun on my heel and sprinted to the door. I ran out of the kitchen, through the shop, and onto the street. I needed to find those clues, and the killer, now more than ever.

CHAPTER 6

The old brick buildings pressed together like whispering neighbors, creating a narrow alley that resembled a badger hole, effectively blocking out the night sky. I strode forward and stopped beneath a rusty fire escape where Forneus claimed the merry dancer had met her demise. I rubbed the back of my neck and kicked at a piece of soiled newspaper. Not a pleasant place to die.

Wind whistled down the alley carrying the rotting tang of garbage and the copper scent of blood. What if Marvin lay crumpled in an alley like this? Was he alive, dead, or injured? The kid had been through so much already in his short life.

I jumped as a hand settled on my shoulder.

"You shouldn't let people sneak up on you," Jinx said.

I gasped and stepped away, letting my friend's hand drop to her side. Crap, Jinx had a point. Nobody should have been able to approach me unawares. Not only had Jinx, a human, entered the alley without my knowing, she'd gotten close enough to touch me. I shivered against the cold. My worry over Marvin was a potentially fatal distraction.

"And you shouldn't be here," I said with a shrug.

"Someone has to keep you on your toes," she said. "You sounded like a crazy person when you called the office. So I decided to close early and meet you here. I know how much the troll kid means to you."

"When I phoned to tell you I was coming here, it wasn't an invitation," I said. "Anyway, I'm working the case. If I find Marvin in the process, all the better."

"Face it," Jinx said. "You have a soft spot for strays."

"I do not," I said. I turned away from Jinx's knowing gaze and examined the ground at my feet. I had moved a nest of pookas into my old tree house and a family of gnomes into my parents' garden, but that had been necessary. Helping to relocate the homeless fae had been the practical thing to do, in both cases. "I just don't like seeing kids get hurt"

"Sure, you just keep telling yourself that," she said. Jinx moved closer, leaning forward to look over my shoulder. "You find anything?"

"Looks like blood," I said. I grabbed one of the pencils from my belt and scraped at the ground. A layer of red ice broke away from the dirty pavement and I swallowed hard. "Kaye thinks our killer may be using blood magic."

"Well that's not disturbing or anything," Jinx said, pointing at the red, ice covered slush. "You've successfully ruined frozen strawberry margaritas for me."

"I didn't ask you to be here," I said. I let out a sigh and stood. I turned in a circle, scanning the brick walls and shadowed doorways. "Come on. We might as well find out if anyone saw anything."

"That could be a waste of time, especially since humans can't see through glamour," she said. "Isn't there a faster way to get clues?"

I ran a gloved hand through my hair and let out a shaky sigh. My eyes cut to the frozen puddle of blood. Sure, there was a faster way, but it could also turn me into a raving lunatic. I usually put off touching the remains of dead things as a last resort.

I shoved my hands into my coat pockets and hunched against the wind. Something small and hard hit the tips of my gloved fingers, and with a crinkle of cellophane, I pulled the item from my pocket. A honey flavored candy sat on my gloved palm.

Damn. I wiped at my face with my sleeve as the chill air tried to freeze the tears that soaked my eyelashes. I should have been buying candy with Marvin. Instead, I was considering touching a frozen puddle of blood in a dirty alley, and Marvin was missing.

Happy freaking holidays.

"Yes, there is a faster way," I said, shuffling forward. "But I'll need your help."

"Sure, what do you need?" she asked.

I unwound my scarf and handed it to Jinx.

"If I start screaming, shove that in my mouth," I said. Her eyes widened, but Jinx nodded. "And if I don't stop screaming, pull me away from the blood…and wash it off my hands."

"Got it," she said.

Jinx forced a brave smile to her lips, but I could see the fear in her eyes. She knew what I wasn't saying. This method may be faster than pounding the pavement and rattling some cages, but it was much more dangerous. There was no guarantee that removing the blood would break the connection.

I looked down at the candy in my hand. The decision was a no-brainer. If the vision got its hooks in me deep enough, I wouldn't be coming back. But if we didn't find Marvin soon, neither would he.

I knelt in the filthy slush of the alley, ignoring the ice cold water that seeped through my pants. It was time to find our killer, and bring Marvin home.

I took a deep breath and pulled my gloves off, one finger at a time. I felt naked and was glad for Jinx's steady presence at my back. If anyone had to see me like this, at least it was the one person I knew I could trust.

I stared at my bare hands and the frozen red liquid just inches away. What was about to come next wouldn't be pretty. Hopefully, Jinx would keep me quiet enough to avoid any curious cops or passerby. If we were up on Joysen Hill, where vamps and other beasties routinely hunt, screams from a dark alley would be commonplace. Too bad we were on the edge of the Old Port. The last thing we needed was a tourist stumbling in and witnessing my bizarre investigation methods. I shook my head, banishing thoughts of screaming bystanders and police interrogations. I'd just have to put my faith in Jinx.

I plunged my right hand into the ice and gasped at the cold as it burned against my skin. I closed my eyes against the image of frozen blood touching my hand. Seconds later, the black of my eyelids was replaced with the image of a dying faerie. I had shifted from reality to a vision and the images were coming in full bloody Technicolor.

And the vision was coming from the perspective of the killer—oh goodie.

Warm liquid ran over my hands from the slashed neck of a merry dancer. I held a ceremonial knife to the faerie's throat and whispered guttural words in a foreign tongue. Scarlet threads of power rose from the body in radiant tendrils to twine up my legs and arms. I felt drunk on the rush of power as I drank the faerie's remaining life essence.

I staggered to my left, leaning against the brick wall of the alley. I steadied my hold on the faerie and the ritual blade in my blood slick hand. My eyes flicked down to the skeleton bundled in my cloak, resting in the shadows.

"Soon my beloved," I whispered.

I continued the incantation, careful to guide the stream of blood along the blade into the bottle nestled in the palm of my hand. The crystal bottle gleamed red and gold with an inner fire and thick black and scarlet smoke rose from within to swirl around the bottle's mouth. The magic was working.

Blood dripped into the bottle as I chanted, filling it to the brim. With a satisfied grin, I used the stopper to seal the bottle tight. But my spell was not the only thing that required blood. It was time to leave payment for those who serve me.

I shifted the weight of the body in my arms, letting the head loll back to expose the drying wound. I drew my blade across the faerie's throat, making a second incision. A small trickle of blood flowed and I held the body out to dangle above the icy ground. Blood dripped and pattered onto the cold pavement, forming a steaming puddle.

The last drop of blood fell to the ground and I threw the body in a heap against the wall. My minions would dispose of it later. Holding my gore covered hands to the sky, I laughed. My power was growing and the day of the ritual was fast approaching. I had the tree and the blood. All was going according to plan.

I pulled a sprig of mistletoe from my pocket and flung it at the exsanguinated body. As if bleeding the immortal dry was not enough, the red caps would be certain to feast on its flesh before carrying the remains to the ritual fire. The kiss of death, indeed. I laughed again, walking jauntily away.

As the killer moved further from the blood cooling on the ground, my perspective shifted. I was no longer looking out through the twisted killer's eyes, but the new view wasn't much of an improvement.

Slinking away from the congealing puddle was a beautiful female faerie. She was obviously not afflicted by the cold as she prowled happily with bare feet across the icy ground. Her pale limbs moved with the lithesome grace of a ballerina. The faerie sashayed to a dramatic halt beside the bundle of bones resting on the ground.

She cocked one long finger at the skeleton, beckoning for him to join her. When the skeleton did not respond, because, hello, he was dead as a doornail, the faerie scooped him up into her arms. The cloak fell to the ground as she twirled the naked skeleton in a macabre parody of lively merriment. But the thing she embraced was long dead and the cruel curl of her lips lacked the warmth of happiness.

"Soon all shall witness your talent again, my love," she said. The faerie sighed, tilting her head of brilliant red hair and frowning playfully. "You were always the most gifted of all of my human pets. Now their art appears garish to my eyes and their music discordant to my ears. Return to me, my sweet, and we shall create beauty together once again."

The faerie spun a graceful pirouette, turning her face toward the spot above the blood puddle where my consciousness hovered. I gasped. The otherwise beautiful woman had empty eyes that seemed to radiate blackness darker than the night around us. As she leaned in to gaze at her skeletal lover, lines of darkness spread further across her face.

Whatever spellwork she was dabbling with, it wasn't doing her any favors.

The faerie gave the skeleton a passionate kiss that made my stomach roil then skipped away, melting into the shadows.

I gasped, the killer and her gruesome vision were gone, but I remained trapped within the psychic impressions left on the blood. I was tethered to the dark, red puddle and nothing I tried would cut me free.

That, of course, was when the nightmare vision went from twisted to absolutely terrifying.

One by one, the alley filled with redcaps. They surrounded the puddle of blood, licking their lips with worm-like tongues. I tried again to break free of the vision and failed.

Redcaps normally live in remote locations, within the ruins of old castles and stone towers. In the North East, they had settled along the coast in abandoned lighthouse towers and crumbling civil war fortifications. Redcaps don't normally live in cities, or stray far from their nest, but I had run into one last summer, literally, while walking the streets of Harborsmouth.

My redcap encounter had been in broad daylight, another aberration since the small, dwarflike fae were nocturnal. But that wasn't the most unusual part of that meeting. After wounding me, the redcap had run his tongue along his evil, black blade. But upon tasting my blood, the creature had bowed to me and apologized, even gifting me his dagger as compensation for his actions. He'd run off too quickly for me to get answers, but Kaye still grumbled whenever she looked at that blade. The encounter remained a puzzle.

Redcaps shouldn't be in the city. But now there were a dozen of the vile creatures dipping their hats into the puddle of blood that the female faerie had left behind. These must be her servants, though who knows what redcaps were good for. I really didn't want to know.

Sadly, I had a ringside seat for the show.

Once the redcaps had each soaked their hat in blood, they surrounded the merry dancer's body. An individual with a particularly large hat lifted the sprig of mistletoe from the corpse and dangled it in the air with a mocking grin. Blood ran down his face, from the cap on his head, as he bent down to kiss the dead faerie. The others leaned in as well, looking for all the world as if they were giving the deceased a departing kiss, but when they came away chunks of flesh were missing from the body.

I'd seen enough.

The merry dancer had been killed as part of a blood magic ritual and red caps were involved. I didn't know what it meant, but I did know now what I needed to do. I had to find the faerie mage's lair, and fast.

I fought against the vision, gagging as the image of feasting redcaps swam before me. *Come on Jinx. Get me the Hell out of here.* The redcaps dove their heads back to the body like blood-crazed piranha, and I screamed. I fought against the vision, becoming more exhausted as I thrashed against the barriers that had grabbed hold of my mind.

It would be so easy to stop fighting, but giving in to the fatigue and despair was not an option. Not only was being trapped in this vision my worst nightmare, but I was no use to Marvin like this. The kid needed my help. Oh Oberon's eyes, I can't give up now.

My muffled screams turned to moans and whimpers as I returned to myself. I gagged and pulled the scarf from my mouth. Bile rose in my throat and I took a deep breath, but my stomach continued to churn. Heaving, I crawled away from the puddle of blood, now frozen, and vomited up my breakfast. Oh yeah, I was never having flavored coffee again.

"Here," Jinx said. Jinx unsealed a sanitizing wipe packet and handed me the wipe and my gloves. "You okay?"

I didn't feel okay, but nodded anyway. No sense making Jinx worry. My friend had managed to wash the blood from my hands, helping to pull me from my vision. I shuddered. That was one nightmare I never wanted to experience again.

I pulled on my gloves and put a hand to my stomach. I waited for the waves of nausea and dizziness to pass. The headache, apparently, was here to stay. I'd kill for an aspirin, but my pockets were full of charms and weapons, not normal things like aspirin and chewing gum.

I stood slowly and looked around the alley. The filthy street had returned to its pre-vision appearance. No redcaps or crazy homicidal mages—thank Mab.

It was also damned cold.

I rubbed my gloved hands over my arms and stamped my feet against the icy pavement. I winced as the sound echoed up and down the alley. My head felt like it was going to split open and the sound of pixies buzzed in my ear, but we didn't have time to waste. Marvin was missing and I had new information on our killer.

It was time for another visit with our local witch.

CHAPTER 7

"Darkness and light, girl," Kaye said, glowering at me. "When you get yourself into a pickle, you do so with both feet now don't you?" Kaye turned to examine Jinx's injuries, a bloodied knee from a fall on the ice, frown lines deepening. "And you, can't you go one day without harming yourself?"

Jinx winced as Kaye roughly slapped a poultice on her skinned knee. Jinx was always getting injured, and Kaye was a talented herbalist and healer, but the two didn't mix well on a good day. With Kaye grumping about what we discovered in the alley, Jinx had found herself in the hot seat. As soon as Kaye turned her attention to me, Jinx limped away toward the hearth where Hob was pretending not to eavesdrop.

"Someone is killing faeries, and using blood magic...and Marvin is missing," I said, tossing my gloved hands in the air. "What was I supposed to do, go home?"

Kaye sighed, letting go of some of her bluster. The old woman seemed to shrink with the motion, making her look tired and frail.

"You're right, dear," she said. "But Leanansídhe? I didn't think I'd see the day that faerie witch walked into my city. And from what you saw in your vision, she's the reason the redcaps are here too."

I'd met a redcap and knew they were something to fear, especially if the evil dagger-wielding monsters came in large numbers, but Leanansídhe wasn't a name I was familiar with.

"Who, or what, is Leanansídhe?" I asked.

"Leanansídhe is a powerful faerie who lures men with her beauty and the promise of artistic success," Kaye said. "The Fairy Mistress, as she is sometimes known, has appeared throughout history. She is the perfect muse, bringing musicians and artists to new heights."

"But?" I asked.

I knew there was a catch. With faerie magic, there was always a catch.

"She lifts them up, but when they crash, they die," Kaye said, nodding. "Leanansídhe feeds off the frenzied life essence of her artist lovers, causing them to waste away. Not that her pets wouldn't end up dead anyway. Her very presence makes men unstable, especially human males. The talent of these men may burn brightly, but there is a cost to burning a candle at both ends. When Leanansídhe tires of them, as she often does, her pets kill themselves rather than live without her. Leanansídhe is the reason why so many rising talents die young."

The faerie bitch sounded like a succubus, or a psychic vamp with benefits. And now she was acting crazy, or crazier than usual, wanting to bring one of her lovers back from the dead.

"Is she a necromancer?" I asked.

Kaye bit her lip and frowned.

"Not exactly," she said. "Leanansídhe's magic has always been used to improve someone else's creativity. But in some cases, of extreme writer's block for example, it could be said that she brought the artist's talent back from the dead. If her desire is great enough, and she is fueling her magic with blood and amplifying it with mistletoe, then it may be possible. Leanansídhe may indeed have the power to raise the dead."

I shivered, an oily sensation swimming across my gut, as I recalled Leanansídhe slipping her skeletal lover some tongue. Oh yeah, she had plenty of desire alright. I shook my head and tried to remember something helpful from my vision.

"Leanansídhe mentioned 'the tree' and being nearly ready," I said. "Do you think she meant the hamadryad's tree?"

"Yes," she said. "I believe the tree and the timing are just as significant as the blood she's been gathering. What do you know of the winter solstice?"

"Isn't that when you're throwing your nudie party?" Jinx asked. Hob snickered over her shoulder.

I winced, flinching under Kaye's glare.

"It's the pagan holiday that the Christians appropriated for their Christmas, right?" I asked.

"Near enough," she said. "The winter solstice has been celebrated by man since Neolithic times, though the fae and other immortal races have acknowledged the significance of the solstice for millennia. It is the longest night of the year and a time of great magical power. Many have reveled in the darkness, while others have celebrated the winter solstice as a time of rebirth, noting the ever lengthening days that follow in its wake. Whether calling upon the darkness or worshiping the rebirth of the sun, practitioners come together as power gathers."

"So, it would be the perfect time to use dark magic to raise the dead," I said. A night of power, darkness, and rebirth—sounded like a necromancer's wet dream.

"Yes," Kaye said. "If Leanansídhe plans to resurrect her lover, the celestial calendar would be in her favor. There is also the mention of the tree. Many traditions include the burning of the Yule log in winter solstice celebrations. This comes from a very old ritual for harnessing power. In ancient times, a hamadryad's tree was sacrificed to the fire. The tree would burn for twelve days, all the while a spell was cast and animal sacrifices were made, and on the twelfth night the magic was released and the spell complete."

"Are you saying that the Twelve Days of Christmas comes from some tree burning, goat sacrificing ritual?" Jinx asked.

Jinx rolled her eyes, obviously not buying Kaye's story. But I'd seen Kaye's power and perused her library. I believed her.

"Then the murders have all been part of Leanansídhe's plan," I said, putting the pieces together. Finally, the killings made sense. "She needed their blood to amplify the spell and their bodies for the sacrificial fire."

Not that there was a lot left of their bodies to sacrifice, after the redcaps filled their bellies.

"And the hamadryad's tree to fuel the fire," Kaye said, nodding. Leanansídhe had killed two faeries with one stone with that murder, gaining the hamadryad for sacrifice and the tree for the ritual fire. "Leanansídhe must be stopped before the twelfth night. Once she is at the pinnacle of her power, the Faerie Mistress will be unstoppable."

Right, and what was to stop the crazy bitch from bringing back all of her dead pets? If she'd been alive for as long as Kaye said, then that was a lot of frenzied lovers. If Leanansídhe wasn't stopped, she'd have an army of zombies by Christmas.

And Marvin could be her next sacrificial lamb.

"What do I need to do?" I asked.

I thrust my chin out and dug in my heels. This Leanansídhe bitch had to be stopped and I was going to be the one to do it. If there was any chance of saving Marvin, then I was all in.

I snuck a glance at Jinx. Worry lines wrinkled her brow, but she nodded. My friend wasn't going to try to talk me out of this job. Good thing, since I'd already decided to rescue Marvin. I wasn't going to let the kid down.

The back door slammed open and we all gasped. Well, speak of the devil.

Jinx yelped and bumped her head on the mantelpiece. Fortunately for her, Hob was too busy staring at the large figure in the doorway to scold her for marring his hearth. I just stood there gaping like a grindylow out of water.

Marvin scratched his cheek and tilted his head to the side as he glanced around the room. His other hand, I noticed, was behind his back. What the heck was going on?

"Marvin, be a dear and explain where you've been," Kaye said. "Ivy has been looking all over the city for you. You were supposed to go shopping together."

Marvin rubbed his head shyly and looked away.

"Sorry, Ivy," he said.

The shock of Marvin being alive, and whole, and *here* was wearing off. I blinked away tears and smiled.

"That's okay, kid," I said. I'm just glad you're alright."

"But where have you been?" Jinx asked, leaning in to examine the troll more closely.

Sweat beaded on Marvin's brow and he stepped back. Marvin looked ready to run.

"Secret," he said, shaking his head.

Marvin had secrets? That was news to me. The kid was like an open book.

"Give us a moment," Kaye said, shooing us away.

Hob slipped down into his home below the hearthstone and I headed out to the hallway. Jinx shrugged and followed. The door closed behind her with a whoosh of magic. Apparently, Kaye wanted some privacy while she interrogated Marvin about where he'd been.

"Think she'll chew him out?" she asked.

"I feel bad for him if she does," I said. "I wouldn't want Kaye mad at me."

"She's not so scary," she said, shrugging and looking at her nails.

"Really?" I asked. "Kaye could destroy your entire shoe collection with the snap of her fingers."

Jinx shuddered. "Okay, that's scary." She slumped against the plain, white wall of the hallway, tilted her head back, and shook thick bangs from her eyes. "Where do you think he was all that time?"

"I don't know," I said with a sigh. "I'm just glad he's safe."

"You going to stick with the case, now that Marvin's back?" she asked.

I thought about lovesick zombies roaming the streets of Harborsmouth, trying to please their Queen.

"Yeah, but you should go home," I said.

"I'm not going home," she said. Jinx pouted and crossed her arms. "I can help."

I tried to think of a reason for Jinx to be somewhere far away from redcaps, blood magic, and a sex-crazed faerie muse turned necromancer.

"Think of all the clients we're losing with no one back at the office to answer the phones," I said. Jinx was obsessed with our business success. Maybe that could work to my advantage. "You can switch the lines to take calls from the loft. It'll be safer there..." She frowned at me. "...and you know how Forneus hates our apartment wards."

"True," she said. "I guess I could work from the loft. But are you sure you won't need my help tracking down this Leanansídhe chick?"

"I'm good," I said, crossing my fingers. "I've got Kaye to help me find Leanansídhe, but I need you to hold Private Eye together and keep our clients happy."

"Okay," she said. "But I'm just a phone call away. Ring me if you need anything."

"Sure thing," I said.

Jinx swung her scarf over her shoulder and sauntered away. At the end of the hall, she stopped and turned back.

"And if you get yourself killed, I'll be the one using necromancy to bring you back to life, so I can kill you myself," she said.

With a final flip of her hair, Jinx was gone. I let out a sigh of relief. One friend, at least, would be safe. Now it was time to find out why Marvin was keeping secrets. I rapped on the kitchen door and walked back inside.

Kaye loomed over Marvin who sat on a low stool, looking chagrined. I winced and hoped that the lecture was over. I didn't want to get between Kaye and her target.

"Come in, Ivy," Kaye said.

She didn't turn to see who was standing in her kitchen, but somehow she knew it was me. I never knew with Kaye if it was magic or good instincts, but no one can sneak up on her. Not that I've ever tried. I'm impatient, but I'm not suicidal.

I waved to Marvin and leaned against the large plank table that took up most of the hearth side of the room. The kitchen, surrounded by Kaye's magic circle, was modern and bright, but the hearth area reminded me of an old pub. Not surprising with a brownie in charge of domestic duties. In fact, I wondered where the little guy was hiding. The old coot wasn't usually timid—he had a badger's short temper and the mind of an imp.

A flash of brown caught my eye, moving along the shelf by Marvin's elbow. Sneaky little bugger. Marvin was still holding something behind his back and Hob was trying to get a look. I shook my head. Curiosity would get the best of a brownie every time.

"That's enough, Hob," Kaye said, spearing the brownie with her stare. "Now, Marvin, I know you wanted your gift to be a surprise, but Ivy has had a bad day. Perhaps you could give her your present early?"

Hob's eyes bugged out at the mention of a gift, but he remained where he was. *Smart brownie.*

Marvin swallowed and held a small bundle out before him. In his large hand was a beautiful pair of gloves.

"For me?" I asked. I sniffed and wiped at the back of my eyes with my sleeve. Jeesh, the wind had been really cold in that alley. Hopefully, I wasn't getting sick.

Marvin nodded and a red hue rose to his cheeks. I stepped forward, but hesitated. Clothing was tricky, since it went against my bare skin, and gloves were the most difficult. If there was a nightmare vision attached to these gloves, I could end up a drooling mess for the holidays. But Marvin was my friend, and I was the closest thing to family the kid had.

I reached out and gingerly lifted the gloves from his palm, trying to smooth a smile across my face.

"Thanks, big guy," I said. I took a deep breath and pulled off the glove I was wearing and slipped one of the new ones on. It fit...like a glove. And there were no horrible visions attached. In fact, there was something about the gloves that felt familiar.

"Marvin went to a lot of trouble to have those made especially for you," Kaye said. "Clurichauns are drunkards and fools, but their tailoring skills rival the infamous cobbler skills of their leprechaun cousins."

I now owned clurichaun crafted gloves? I smiled. That was kind of cool.

"Too drunk for bad thoughts," Marvin said, nodding.

"Yes, clurichauns remain much too inebriated to leave unhappy energy or focused visions on their wares," Kaye said. "And Marvin was clever. He asked Jinx for a piece of leather from an old coat you were donating to Goodwill. That way the material itself would not harm you either."

I always knew that Marvin was smarter than he looked. Now I was convinced the kid was a genius.

"Wow, that's brilliant, Marvin," I said. I flashed the kid a smile. "Thanks. These are the best present ever."

For the first time in years, I actually meant it. Too bad I couldn't revel in the happy moment.

"So," I said, turning to Kaye. "Any idea how I can track down this Leanansídhe bitch before the solstice?"

Unfortunately, Kaye did have an idea. I just didn't like it much. Great, another scary fae to track down. Why does it always have to be a hag?

CHAPTER 8

I kicked a chunk of ice from the edge of the curb and yelped. Taking my frustration out on the frozen landscape wasn't helping. If I hadn't been wearing steel toe boots, I'd be nursing a broken foot.

I stuffed gloved hands into my coat pockets and kept my head down as I continued up the darkening street. I was entering the financial district, a small, but prosperous section of the city hemmed in by corporate glass monstrosities. Looking up at the skyscrapers only gave me vertigo, so I kept my eyes at street level.

The wrought iron and cobbled streets of the Old Port had been replaced by ugly chrome and concrete. Every block of the financial district looked the same with its glossy, high-end boutiques, towering law offices, and a Starbucks on every corner.

"We're not in Kansas anymore," I muttered.

"No, you are in Harborsmouth," a familiar voice rumbled from the shadows. "But, then, you knew that already."

I turned to see Forneus emerge from the doorway of a large insurance company. He ran a hand down his expensive suit and fell into step beside me. I sidled away, prepared to run into the sea of rush hour traffic flowing up Congress Street if it meant avoiding his touch.

"What are you doing here?" I asked. I stopped walking and spun to face him, tapping my foot.

"Working," Forneus said. He spread his arms and gestured at the glass and concrete buildings that lined the street. "A demon has to harvest souls somewhere. And contrary to popular belief, lawyers and insurance agents do indeed have souls to sell."

Great. Forneus was down here playing Let's Make A Deal with corporate workaholics while I froze my butt off trying to find a certain faerie hag. Something cold and wet found its way down the neck of my coat and I shivered. It wasn't fair.

As we stood on the sidewalk, snowflakes fell around Forneus, but never managed to land on the demon.

"Don't let Kaye find out you're down here stealing souls," I said. I narrowed my eyes and gripped a silver cross in my gloved hand. In my other pocket, I scooped up a palm full of salt.

"Steal?" he asked. "You wound me deeply, Miss Granger. I can assure you that any deal I make is legally sound."

Yeah, right, and I'm the son of Oberon.

"Look, you were right about the killings," I said. "Someone is murdering faeries. So I don't have time to stand around here and grow icicles. I'll see you around, Forneus."

"Wait," he said. "I know the location of the one you seek."

"Leanansídhe?" I asked.

"Ah, so that is who has been killing faeries," he said. "No, sadly I do not know where to find the Faerie Mistress, but I can lead you to the Winter Hag."

Crap. Forneus had known about the Winter Hag, but not Leanansídhe. Sneaky demon bastard.

"What makes you think I'd trust you?" I asked. "I'm not making a deal for information. No dates with Jinx, remember?"

"You trusted my information about the killer," he said, grinning. "As for the location of The Cailleach, take it as a token of my friendship."

Friendship? With a demon? I laughed.

"You have to be kidding," I said. "What's in it for you, really?"

Forneus sighed and I held my breath as the smell of sulfur filled the street.

"Fine," he said, straightening his tie. "I may have a tidy sum riding on the outcome of this case. But such trivial details do not matter. Find the Winter Hag and stop the killings. She can be found gathering wood and feeding the deer in the park."

Forneus pointed in the direction of Founders Park. When Kaye said she sensed the magic of the Winter Hag in the financial district, I'd never thought to check the park. My friend had described The Cailleach as a strong elemental force who was often referred to as the Queen of Winter, though not to be mistaken with Mab herself. I assumed the hag must have been some corporate president or CEO—an ice queen in her glass tower.

Instead, she sounded like one of the homeless who called Founders Park their home.

I turned back to Forneus, but the demon had disappeared. Whatever. I shrugged and hurried down the sidewalk to where Congress Street was bisected by Park Avenue. The financial district had emptied during my talk with Forneus and Park Ave was devoid of any human presence. The only sign of life being the well lit Starbucks on the corner.

I could go for a real cup of coffee, especially after the nasty stuff Jinx had served this morning, but it was already getting late. I needed to find The Cailleach before midnight. Magic users weren't the only ones whose power grew during the Witching Hour and Kaye had warned me that the Winter Hag was a cyclical force that waxed and waned with the seasons and the hours of the day. I wanted information, not to find myself on the receiving end of a transformation spell. Becoming one of The Cailleach's pet deer was not part of my plan.

I shivered and hurried down the street, careful not to slip on the icy sidewalk. Congress Street ran on a high ridge, the backbone of the city. Every street that ran away from Congress slanted steeply downwards, and Park Ave was no exception. As I descended toward the park, the harbor wind at my back ceased.

I scanned the street for assailants then shifted my attention to the park. Crossing the empty street, I warily approached the park entrance. Keeping my charms and makeshift stakes handy, I watched the trees for movement, but the only motion came from flickering shadows beneath a humming streetlight.

Lengthening shadows reached like skeletal fingers as the sun began to set behind the trees. I clutched the iron nails in my pocket and crept forward on the balls of my feet. I searched the darkness below the trees one more time and, satisfied that nothing supernatural lurked there, stepped onto the frozen grass. The gates hung open like a yawning grave and nothing stirred as I entered Founders Park.

It was like entering another world.

The sounds of city life drifted away, replaced by dead air. A heavy silence smothered the park, broken only by a high pitched squeak as a hunched figure came toward me pushing a rusty shopping cart. The sun retreated and the ice covered pond snapped as a thick layer of frozen water shifted. I jumped and the old crone cackled.

I had found The Cailleach.

I cleared my throat and stepped into a pool of light cast by the flickering street lamp. The hag lifted her head and my stomach heaved. A dark socket was all that was left of her right eye. The other eye stared at me over a large, beaklike nose and her skin was an unhealthy shade of blue. The Cailleach was half my height and her body was bent forward under the weight of a large bundle strapped to her back. The stooped position forced the old crone to twist her neck at an uncomfortable angle to look me in the eye.

The Cailleach was completely unlike the water hags I'd dealt with in the past. Hopefully, that meant she was less crazy than her swamp-dwelling cousins.

The Winter Hag lifted a bag of dried corn and flashed a toothless grin.

"Hungry?" she asked.

The old crone was trying to feed me deer food? Okay, maybe she was mad as a hatter.

"Um, no thanks," I said.

I shuffled my feet wondering how to begin. Asking faerie favors was tricky. A faerie bargain was binding and immortality gave the fae a long time to practice their deal making skills. I had learned the hard way that faeries will always get the upper hand. The trick wasn't winning so much as surviving.

And I didn't have time for haggling.

"Too bad," she said. The Cailleach sighed and tucked the bag of corn into the folds of her rag dress. "You would have made a lovely pet."

Mab's bones, she really did want to turn me into one of her pet deer. My chest tightened and I struggled to breathe normally. This wasn't the time for a panic attack. I shook my head and focused on the job. I needed to learn the location of Leanansídhe's lair and get the hell out of Dodge.

"I can bring you more deer food, for information on where I can find Leanansídhe," I said.

I planted my feet hip width apart and took a deep breath. My gloved hands were cramping, but I held tightly to my anti-fae charms. If this went down badly, I'd have to fight or run.

The Cailleach rummaged through her cart, finally finding whatever it was she was looking for.

"This will lead you to the Faerie Mistress," she said. She held out a hotel key in a gnarled hand. "But human food will not sate my pets. If you wish to strike this bargain, I require a branch from the hamadryad's tree. Fetch me a branch before the Yule log fully burns or face my wrath. That is my offer."

Crap, what were the odds that I could do as she asked? But what choice did I have? I needed to find Leanansídhe before she unleashed her zombie lovers on the world. Talk about a Christmas gift from Hell. I lifted my chin and nodded curtly.

"Deal," I said.

The hag raised her hand and cackled, the laugh ending in a phlegm-filled cough. The hotel key fell to the frost covered ground. With a squeak of the rusty cart, The Cailleach lurched away, the bundle of sticks on her back rocking to and fro as she shuffled deeper into the park.

Was the key the clue, or did it require a vision? I skirted the key like a viper, finally hunching down and slipping a glitter topped pencil from my belt. I slid the pencil through the key ring and lifted it to the streetlight. A fancy crest and the words "Bishop Hotel" gleamed dully in the flickering light. I'd sniff around there and see if anyone had seen any suspicious activity. Maybe the Faerie Mistress was staying there and the key led to Leanansídhe's room.

It was a start.

CHAPTER 9

One thing was painfully obvious as I strode up the steps of the Bishop Hotel. No one had occupied a room here in years. The door hung open, the frame swollen and warped from damp and disuse.

I pushed the door open wider with the toe of my boot and peeked inside. Black mold climbed the walls, marring the elaborate wallpaper and draperies. The lobby was lit only by light from the street lamps outside that filtered in through the open door and a broken window gaping above a second-floor balcony.

I flicked on a mini Maglite and shone it around the room. The floor looked sound, though I avoided the decaying carpet runner as I stepped into the room. I covered my face with a gloved hand and stifled a sneeze. Dust rose in amber clouds as I tiptoed further into the hotel lobby.

I shone my light along the floor where small feet had walked back and forth through the dust, a large object dragged between them. Someone, probably Leanansídhe's redcap henchmen, had been here recently.

I followed the tracks, careful not to make a sound as I walked past a marble counter and into a dark service passage. The hallway was wide, but unadorned. An old laundry cart stood beside a metal door farther down the hall to my right and a storeroom spilling its contents into the corridor was to my left.

I stepped over the abandoned bottles of cleaner and rolls of toilet paper that prior thieves hadn't wanted and followed the dusty prints down the hall toward the laundry cart. I stood on tiptoe and peered inside the small window inset into the metal door. Stairs led down into impermeable darkness.

Great, it looked like the redcaps were holing up in the basement. I reached out with a gloved hand and tried the doorknob, surprised when it turned easily. I turned my head to the side and examined the door. It wasn't locked. Leanansídhe was either sloppy or confident that she and her redcaps could deal with any intruders.

Or maybe the faerie was just too crazy to care.

My stomach tensed and I forced myself into motion. Standing in the spooky old hallway wasn't doing me any good. Plus, I had to locate the hamadryad's tree, and remove a branch for The Cailleach, before it burned completely. Sadly, amorous zombies weren't my only worry. If Leanansídhe was successful, and the Yule log burned to ash, I'd have no way of fulfilling my end of the bargain with the Winter Hag. I shivered, icy fingers trailing up and down my spine. That was one old crone I didn't want to break a deal with.

I pulled the metal door open and let the narrow beam from my flashlight shine down the stairway. I gasped and lurched back, distancing myself from the mass of spider webs that clung to the ceiling and walls. The redcaps had come this way, but they were pint-sized compared to my height. The webs had only been cleared as high as my knees.

Why did it always have to be spiders?

A memory of the spider "cloth merchant" on Joysen Hill crept in unbidden. The carnivorous faerie had used his glamour to cover his terrifying visage, and the bodies of his prey, from human eyes. Unfortunately for me, my second sight allowed me to cut through his glamour to see the men and women wrapped in spider silk, hanging from the fire escape above his market stall. The image of wriggling human-sized snacks dangling above the spider faerie had haunted my dreams for weeks.

I swallowed hard and rubbed my gloved hands along my arms. I could do this. There were no man-eating spider fae here. It was just a bunch of old cobwebs, right? I took a shuddering breath and crept down the stairs, moving as fast as I could without alerting the entire basement of my presence.

"It's just cotton candy," I muttered.

Something skittered along a web to my left and I cringed. I pulled the collar of my coat up higher and kept moving. At the bottom of the stairs, I took a shuddering breath and shook web from my hands and hair.

Waiting for my eyes to adjust to the dim light, I studied the smells of mildew, wood smoke, and decay. A hint of detergent hung on the air and I realized the large objects to my far left were washing machines. My eyes continued to adjust to the darkness and I confirmed that this was the laundry room for the hotel. Industrial washers and dryers lined one wall and a large steamer sat like a metal gargoyle in the center of the room.

I crouched down and circuited the steamer and folding tables. Something let out a raucous laugh and tinny chamber music played in the room beyond. I froze, but when no one came looking for me, I continued forward.

Beyond the laundry room was a cavernous space. The walls were rough brick lined with exposed plumbing and wiring for the hotel above. A large furnace was the focal point of the room. The metal beast billowed smoke where it rose from the dirt floor, but someone had tried to make the place homey—if you lived in a Victorian parlor.

I inched further into the room, keeping to the shadows, to get a better view. Velvet fainting couches lined the walls beside small tables covered in doilies and photographs of people sleeping. In coffins? Scratch that, they weren't sleeping. The people in the gilt frames were dead. That wasn't creepy or anything.

But the creep factor didn't stop there. Redcaps surrounded the large furnace. The door of the furnace hung open, a large tree protruding from its fiery maw. The redcaps looked like red ants climbing up and down a series of ropes to where a metal spit hung over the burning tree. Taking turns, the redcaps cranked a lever, turning the items on the spit over and over again.

My stomach roiled and I looked away. The dead faeries—peri, hamadryad, pixie, Fear Dearg, and the merry dancer—hung from the spit as it slowly rotated over the fire. Bile rose in my throat and I swallowed hard. The redcaps giggled with glee each time the bodies snapped and popped above the fire, as if eagerly awaiting a Christmas roast.

I blinked away tears from the lingering smoke haze and scanned the room for additional threats. There, sitting on a striped satin fainting couch was Leanansídhe and her dead lover. The Faerie Mistress cradled the skeleton in her arms, relishing in his embrace. She lifted an athame, ritual dagger, in one hand and dragged it along the skeleton's cheek, then leaned in for a kiss. The macabre tableau made my stomach twist and I felt my skin crawl.

Leanansídhe was most definitely unhinged. As Hob once explained to me, the very, very old fae tended to go through an unhealthy stage of boredom that was often followed by a period of "goin' doolally." Some fae manage to retrieve their sanity again over time, but most remained damaged. I thought Jinx put it best when I explained my earlier vision of the Faerie Mistress. Leanansídhe was fucknuts crazy.

With the powerful faerie and her pets surrounding the Yule log, there was no way that I could retrieve The Cailleach's branch, remove the bodies from the roasting spit, pull the hamadryad's tree from the fire, and put an end to the power fueling the necromancy spell. I needed more firepower.

It was time to call Jenna.

I crept back toward the entrance, holding my breath as I crab-walked back the way I came. I bit my lip, back muscles straining, as I inched forward, careful not to bump the table holding the gramophone. Making the music skip would definitely catch Leanansídhe's attention.

My boots touched concrete and I let out a shaky breath. I'd made it to the laundry room. I risked a glance back to the cavernous room behind me to see the Faerie Mistress continuing to stroke the cheek of her skeleton lover. For now, at least, I was safe.

I scanned the laundry room for threats then inched to the basement stairs. Looking up through the tunnel of spider webs, the door to the hotel looked far away. But I couldn't risk making the call here. I needed to escape the basement level where I might be overheard.

Pulling my coat tight around my neck, I put one foot on the step, then another. I was nearly at the door, my hand reaching for the handle, when a stair tread let out a loud squeak of protest. I lifted my foot and froze. Had I given myself away?

I held my breath and counted to twenty. Sticky webs tickled my nose and something skittered along my coat sleeve. An itch burned between my shoulder blades, but I didn't turn around. When I was sure that there were no footsteps approaching from behind me, I crept up the last few stairs and pushed out into the hotel service corridor.

With trembling hands, I closed the metal door and leaned against it. Mab's bones, that was close. I closed my eyes and took a steadying breath. I made a mental note of which stair had had the squeaky tread and pushed away from the wall.

It was time to call in reinforcements.

I punched in Jenna's number from memory. The petite, young Hunter had helped me on a few cases since we'd met last summer. We weren't exactly friends—she killed faeries for a living and I was a wisp half-breed—but I'd earned her respect that first night on the waterfront. I had been ready to die to save innocent humans from supernatural baddies and that was what all Hunters were sworn to do. I may not be fully human myself, but I fit with Jenna's ideals. So far that worked for both of us.

"Got a case?" Jenna asked. Her breathless voice came down the line in bits and pieces between the rhythmic clang of metal on metal. She must have been in the sparring room at the Guild's home base, where Hunters trained obsessively. "Just a sec." The background noise ceased and Jenna let out a barking laugh. "Need help with another gnome infestation?"

I grimaced. Jenna had helped me net a small family of gnomes long enough to warn them that the empty lot where they lived was being turned into a shopping mall. My client had hired me to serve the eviction notice. It had sounded like a straightforward job, but the gnomes had cried and pleaded with me. It hadn't been my finest moment.

"Not gnomes, redcaps," I said, keeping my voice low. "And a faerie necromancer. I'm at the old Bishop Hotel on Forsythe. Leanansídhe and her redcap minions are down in the basement. I need to stop a blood magic spell that she's casting, but so far they've only harmed other faeries..."

"So the Guild won't help on this one," she said.

The Hunters Guild only helped fight against faeries to protect humans. Since Leanansídhe hadn't hurt any humans yet, their hands were tied. But Jenna wasn't opposed to the occasional side job. She said it kept her skills sharp.

Personally, I didn't think Jenna needed the practice, but I was always happy to have her help. I kept in shape and went through a series of self-defense moves each evening while Jinx made dinner, but I used speed and surprise to disarm and run away from my attackers. Hand to hand combat was no good when the brush of skin on skin could mean crippling visions. Jenna had offered to teach me how to handle a blade, but even the thought of holding a weapon made my stomach hurt.

"Right, the Guild isn't an option," I said. "Are you in?"

"Be there in five," she said. "And Ivy? Don't do anything foolish before I get there."

I considered the basement full of bloodthirsty redcaps and their crazy, magic using faerie leader.

"That won't be a problem," I said. "I'll wait for you in the lobby."

CHAPTER 10

Five minutes seemed to take an eternity, but Jenna arrived on schedule. She may spend most of her time plotting to kill faeries, but Jenna was punctual. You had to give her that.

"We have approximately nine redcaps here," Jenna said. She made a mark in the dust that covered the lobby floor. "And you last saw the faerie mage here."

"Yes," I said, nodding at the hasty diagram.

"Okay," she said. "You go in first and I'll bring up the rear. Get as close to the furnace as you can, without the redcaps seeing you. Once you're in close, I'll create a distraction. Run to the Yule log and retrieve the branch you need from the tree. After securing the branch, hit the emergency shutdown switch here. That should cut off the oil supply, but with wood to fuel the fire, the tree will probably continue to burn. Loop the rope around the tree and try to pull it from the furnace. I'll come over and help once I incapacitate the enemy."

Jenna made it sound easy, but I had a bad feeling that we were taking on something too big for just the two of us. I was tempted to call Kaye for magical support, but shook away the thought. The fight on the waterfront had weakened Kaye physically and diminished her power. I thought of the black lines snaking down my friend's arms to encircle her wrists and hands. I sat up straight and clenched my fist. No, I wasn't going to put Kaye in danger again. She may not survive another magic battle. Jenna and I would have to do this on our own.

"Anything else?" I asked.

"If you see anything hiding beneath a glamour that I don't, text me," she said. "I'll have my phone on vibrate. If it looks like I'm about to walk into a glamoured trap, scream bloody murder. Otherwise, stick with the plan."

Jenna didn't have my gift of second sight, but Hunters don't run blindly into battle. Jenna's eyelids shone with a greasy substance she'd rubbed on when she got here. Faerie ointment didn't work as well as second sight, but it did help humans see glamoured fae.

The scent of faerie ointment—clover, periwinkle, culver's keys, forget-me-nots, primrose, and thyme—reminded me of Jinx. Kaye had whipped up a batch when our clientele had changed. Being able to tell if the person walking through your office door was a creature that may want to eat you tended to be helpful, though Jinx applied hers with a makeup brush. Jenna looked like she was suffering from a bad case of conjunctivitis.

I felt a pang of guilt when I thought about my roommate. I hadn't called Jinx to tell her that I'd found Leanansídhe's lair. My friend would have rushed here in an effort to keep me safe. Jinx was tough, but she wasn't a Hunter. It was better that she was safe back at the loft. Now we just had to stop the bad guys and keep her that way.

"Okay, ready when you are," I said.

I brushed dust from my knees and led Jenna down the service corridor. Having a sudden idea, I stopped at the open supply closet and poked my head inside. There on the bottom shelf was a first aid kit and a fire extinguisher. I moved the first aid kit, and a stack of towels, out into the hallway where we might need them later. The fire extinguisher I lifted up to show Jenna and grinned.

"What do you think?" I asked. "If I douse the wood after hitting the manual shut off for the furnace, this should put the fire out. We may not have to pull the Yule log out of the furnace."

I'd been worrying about that detail. I wanted to zip in and out, foiling the Faerie Mistress' plans by ruining her spell. If I didn't have to waste time dragging an entire tree from a furnace, I'd have a chance to save the remains of the faeries who had died at the hands of Leanansídhe and her redcap cronies.

"Check the last charge date," she said.

I turned the extinguisher over and, miraculously, it hadn't expired. The propellant and fire retardant were good for another month.

"Looks good," I said.

"Then bring it," she said. "If it gets too unwieldy, leave it and keep moving. Stealth will be the most important thing. You need to get close to the furnace before I begin my diversion."

I nodded, patting the fire extinguisher and tucking it under my arm. I went to the metal basement door and peeked through the tiny window pane to the stairs below. I didn't shine my flashlight this time. It was dark, but I couldn't detect any movement on the stairs.

I pulled the door open and began my descent, careful to avoid the squeaky step. Jenna followed my lead and I turned my attention back to the shadowy basement below. Once we'd cleared the stairs, I crouched low and crab-walked through the laundry room. I passed the looming steamer press with Jenna at my back. So far, so good.

My boots hit dirt and I peered around the corner into the cavernous room beyond. I bit my lip and scanned the room for faeries. Leanansídhe was dancing with her skeleton in the center of the dirt floor. But where were the redcaps?

I jumped at the loud squeal of rusting hinges as the door of every washer and dryer snapped opened behind us. Teeth and daggers gleamed red in the faint firelight as redcaps emerged from where they'd been hiding inside the bellies of the machines. Oh Oberon's eyes, we had walked into a redcap ambush.

I froze, watching redcaps pour out of the machines like spiders in a rainstorm. For creatures with short, stubby legs, they sure could move fast.

Jenna spun on her heel to face our ambushers and shouted, "Ivy, go!"

I launched out of my crouch, stealth no longer an option, and ran toward the burning Yule log. We had abandoned our original plan, forced by the attack to improvise, but my goal remained the same. I had to shut down the furnace and stop the tree from burning.

With no redcaps in my path, I sprinted past the gramophone and over an ornate fainting couch. The sounds of battle raged behind me, but I couldn't risk looking over my shoulder. I had to stick with my goal. But redcaps were nasty little creatures and I hoped that Jenna would be able to fight them off long enough for me to disrupt Leanansídhe's spell.

I smiled as I heard the *thwap, thwap* of Jenna's crossbow, followed by a ragged scream. The Hunter had hit one of the redcaps with an iron bolt. That was one bloodthirsty faerie who wouldn't be continuing this fight. One redcap down, seven more to go.

The furnace grew larger as I made my way across the room and my chest lightened. Calling Jenna had been the right decision. The clang of her sword rang out and another redcap wailed. We were going to shut this spell down and save the day. No more innocent faeries were going to die. Not in my city.

I grinned, showing my teeth, and increased my speed. My thighs were burning, but I was nearly there. All those morning runs along the waterfront were finally paying off.

A low muttering echoed against the walls off to my right and my grin faltered. Leanansídhe had lowered her skeleton dance partner to the ground and her lips moved rapidly as she recited an incantation. Crap, that was never a good sign.

I turned to see if help was on the way, but Jenna had her hands full with the redcaps.

Their bloodlust had reached a frenzied pitch at the bloodletting of their comrades. The redcaps were climbing over the bodies of their fallen to encircle Jenna. Mab's bloody bones.

I was on my own.

I veered to the right, toward Leanansídhe. I couldn't outrun a spell, but maybe I could toss a monkey wrench into the works. And when you don't have a monkey wrench, a fire extinguisher will do.

I hooked the gloved fingers of my left hand under the spray nozzle and slapped my right hand on the back of the red metal tank. Swinging the fire extinguisher in an arc, I used my momentum to smash the Faerie Mistress in the head—and kept on running.

A jolt of pain ran up my arms, but I retained my grip on the metal canister. I still needed the fire extinguisher if I hoped to put out the flames that continued to eat away at the Yule log. Plus, I might need it again for more head bashing.

I risked a glance over my shoulder as I continued my run for the furnace. Leanansídhe was still standing, but she had stopped mouthing the words of her spell. Knowing it wouldn't last long, I used the brief reprieve to bolt forward and hit the emergency power shutoff button on the side of the furnace.

I wiped tearing eyes with the backs of my gloves and headed into the thick smoke surrounding the Yule log. Pulling my scarf around my nose and mouth, I peered through the haze looking for a branch for The Cailleach.

A scream rang out from behind me, but I focused on what was left of the hamadryad's tree. There, toward the end of the burning log, one branch remained. The tips of the winter-dry branch were beginning to curl in the heat, but it was whole. I breathed a sigh of relief. Surviving this only to be struck down by the Winter Hag would suck, big time.

Leanansídhe's guttural muttering began again and I hurried forward. I brushed sparks from my coat and reached over the blackened tree trunk to grab the branch. I gripped the base of the branch with both gloved hands, but flames roared as the Faerie Mistress pulled power from the burning Yule log to fuel her spell.

No! I fell backward, blinking my eyes against the flames that shot three feet into the air. The hamadryad's tree was burning faster and the remaining branch had caught fire. I had to douse the flames. The burning Yule log and the blood sacrifices hanging above were lending power to Leanansídhe's magic.

The branch would have to wait.

I raised the fire extinguisher and aimed it at the center of the blaze. Once the flames within the furnace began to dim, I swung the extinguisher back toward the burning branch before resuming my attempt to extinguish the flames.

I sensed movement, grabbed a handful of iron shavings from my pocket and flung them at the ground behind me. If it was Jenna the iron wouldn't do her any harm, but the iron would burn any pureblood fae. Judging by the screams, it hadn't been my human friend.

I continued to aim the fire extinguisher at the furnace until, with a final puff and fizzle, the device ran dry. I couldn't see through the cloud of smoke, foam, and white powder, but I heard a growl to my left.

I ducked and rolled beneath the Yule log, where it protruded from the furnace, holding the fire extinguisher to my chest. The growling followed me beneath the tree and I sprung

to my feet the moment I'd cleared it, and swung the metal
canister at knee height—right at head level, for a redcap. I
nearly took the redcap's head off as he ran at the oncoming
battering ram.

The redcap's eyes rolled up into his skull as he fell over
backward. I lifted the fire extinguisher onto my shoulder and
reached inside my coat. I withdrew a packet of powdered
mandrake root and sprinkled it over the burning tree and onto
the floor below. It wouldn't stop the full force of Leanansídhe's
spells, but any protection against black magic was welcome at
this point.

I kicked the redcap, making sure he was out cold, and
surveyed the battle. The room had filled with smoke, making it
difficult to pick out friend or foe. But I couldn't feel the electric
tingle that often accompanied powerful magic.

I moved back toward where I'd last seen the burning
branch, crossing my fingers. If I didn't have a branch for The
Cailleach, I'd be up an *each uisge* filled creek.

I squinted through the smoke and brushed away the
thick layer of foam and white powder that coated the tree,
trunk and branch. Had the remaining branch burned? It was
time to find out. I set the fire extinguisher on the ground at my
feet and reached forward with shaking hands.

My gloved hands found the slender wood sprouting from
the log and brushed away the last of the powder. Brown and
gray bark emerged—the branch was intact. I snapped the
branch from the tree, wrapped it in my scarf, and tucked it into
my belt. The branch created a large bulge beneath my coat,
but I wasn't going to leave it here. I patted the bundle and
smiled.

I could live to fight another day.

The Cailleach may let me live, but I was sure the
redcaps and their mistress had other ideas—if they were still
alive. Boots crunched on iron shavings and I grabbed two
stakes from my belt. They may not work as well on fae as they
would with vamps, but I could certainly slow down a redcap if I
jammed a stake in its eye.

I strained my hearing and held my breath. I blinked
away tears, but couldn't see anything through the heavy
smoke. The steps continued toward me, sounding light and

graceful. I lifted my arm higher and adjusted my grip on the stake. That didn't sound like an approaching redcap.

I counted—one one thousand, two one thousand, three one thousand—and swung my right arm, ready to follow up with my left. A hand lashed out and grabbed my wrist in its iron grip and I tensed, sucking air through my teeth. Receiving a vision from Leanansídhe could fry my brain. I remembered Kaye reciting the immortal Faerie Mistress' long line of pet artists. Leanansídhe had left thousands of corpses in her wake. I bit the inside of my cheek, tamping down my panic. If given the choice, I'd rather face her magic.

The scent of primrose and thyme met my nose and I slumped forward. I loosened my grip on the stakes and locked my knees, trying not to slide to the floor. My legs had gone wobbly, and stars danced on the edge of my vision, but the Hunter's face emerged from the smoke haze.

"Jenna?" I asked.

"If I'd been the Faerie Mistress, you'd be dead right now," Jenna said. She shook her head and let go of my wrist. "You really need to reconsider my offer for weapons training."

I let out a shaky laugh and brushed a piece of falling ash from my cheek. Jenna had a point. I caught a glimpse of my gloves and winced. I was lucky that my hands weren't covered in third-degree burns. My leather gloves were a charred mess. Good thing Marvin had given me new ones for Christmas. I'd have to make sure and thank the kid.

"You may be right," I said. "So where is Leanansídhe?"

Jenna pointed to the ground a few feet away. The faerie was sitting in the dirt, rocking the skeleton she held in her arms. A low moaning rose from her mouth and Leanansídhe began sobbing into the skeleton's shoulder.

"Must hear him play again...such beautiful music," she cried.

I almost felt bad for her. My eyes rose to the small bodies hanging from the spit above the blackened tree. The bodies were charred and covered in bite marks from where Leanansídhe had encouraged the redcaps to feed. Maybe she didn't deserve my pity. I limped to a dainty, velvet armchair and pulled it over to the furnace.

"What do we do with her?" Jenna asked.

Jenna pulled her crossbow from her back and aimed it at the insane faerie. I shrugged. I didn't have a lot of sympathy for Leanansídhe. She'd killed....for her own greed. But she was obviously unhinged. I thought back to the number of times I had come close to losing my own sanity.

Jenna began pulling the bow string back and I shook my head. I may not like the faerie witch, especially now that I was standing eye to eye with her roasted victims, but the woman was clearly insane.

"Wait," I said, raising a smoking hand. "Let me call Kaye. She'll know what to do."

Jenna went back to guarding Leanansídhe and I struggled to dial The Emporium with scorched gloves. Kaye wasn't thrilled at my suggestion to keep the faerie alive, but eventually, she caved in. She knew a Ghillie Dhu who ran a faerie rehab containment facility outside Boston. I was fuzzy on the details, but the important thing was Kaye agreed to make the necessary calls and get Leanansídhe into the facility before dawn. It may have been kinder to kill the faerie, but at least I wouldn't be responsible for her death.

I'd do almost anything to protect my friends and keep the city safe, but I wasn't comfortable with the role of executioner. And if I agreed to let Jenna kill Leanansídhe, that's exactly what I'd be. It didn't matter which of us pulled the trigger.

While talking to Kaye on speakerphone, I worked at removing the dead bodies from the metal spit. I had trudged back up the basement stairs and retrieved the first aid kit and towels from the hotel service corridor. I now had my gloved hands and arms wrapped in towels monogrammed with the BH of the Bishop Hotel. My entire body shook, but I swallowed my fear of nightmare visions and finished the job. Talking with Kaye helped to keep me distracted.

I used gauze from the first aid kit and more towels as shrouds, wrapping each of the burned bodies before setting them on one of the fancy couches that lined the walls. It was hard work, wrapping the faeries with my own clumsy, towel wrapped hands. But they deserved this token of respect. I would make sure that each of the bodies was returned to their people and laid to rest in the manner in which they would wish. It seemed like the least I could do.

I hadn't been able to protect these faeries, but I swore that no more innocents, fae or human, would go unnoticed in my city. Not on my watch. And if I was going to be protecting the residents of Harborsmouth, I needed more training.

"Jenna, that offer for weapons training still stand?" I asked.

Jenna wasn't cheap, but I could give myself training sessions for Christmas. Maybe Jinx would like lessons as well. She was getting feisty with her sharpened crosses and holy water grenades. Making ourselves kick ass for the New Year? Sounded like a resolution to me.

Of course, I'd still have to get Jinx a new pair of shoes. Either that or I'd be the first person she'd stake.

EPILOGUE

My hand twitched as the Felix the Cat clock ticked on the kitchen wall. I scowled at the time and grabbed my shawl from the granite counter, shaking my head. I had hoped that Ceff would be here to escort me to Kaye's crappy solstice party, but he hadn't shown. The kelpie and selkie negotiations must not be going well.

I stomped to the door, and flicked off the overhead lights. I stood in the glow of the city lights that filtered in through the loft windows and took a steadying breath. Jinx had gone on ahead with her date while I insisted on waiting for Ceff.

I should have gone with Jinx and Hans, but I felt like a third wheel and I still wasn't thrilled about Jinx going on a date with the Hunter. Hans was trouble, but then again so was Jinx. I shook my head. At least she wasn't going with Forneus. The demon had sent numerous requests to be her date, but Jinx had refused. At least attending the party on the arm of a skilled Hunter meant that Jinx wouldn't be bothered by the demon tonight. I sighed and leaned against the cool metal of our apartment door.

I'd have to walk into Kaye's party on my own.

I was used to being a loner, but walking into a nude dance party, rife with magic circles and group orgies, had me checking my body for weapons. The dress I'd worn, since I wasn't going to tear off my clothes and run naked under the solstice moon, didn't have as many places for stashing stakes and blades as I'd like. How did Jinx manage to hide all of those sharpened crosses in her skirts?

I snorted, remembering Jinx's last attempt to stab Forneus. Jinx and I had started taking lessons with our Hunter friend Jenna and the training sessions had paid in spades. Too bad demons like the rough stuff. Jinx was never going to rid herself of Forneus now.

I tipped my head back and stared at the ceiling. Maybe I'd feel better after a walk under the stars. Starlight soothed my wisp half and the walk might calm my jangled nerves. If not, I could stop on the way for some liquid courage. The streets between our apartment and The Emporium were lined with bars and it was late on a Wednesday night. I might be able to duck in and out without anyone trying to touch me. And if they tried, I'd have an excuse to use some of the moves Jenna was teaching me.

I grinned, showing my teeth, and pulled the door open. Ceff stood startled on the top landing. His hand was lifted, as if to knock on the door. I gasped and stepped back, but the grin didn't leave my face.

"You made it," I said, looking him over.

Ceff looked dapper in a suit and tie, but if you looked past his faerie glamour he wasn't wearing shoes. Apparently, kelpie kings prefer to go around barefoot, even in winter. I glanced up in time to see Ceff looking me over as well. I blushed, running a hand down the shimmering dress. I had planned on wearing pants and a turtleneck, but Jinx had insisted on the evening gown.

"You look stunning in that dress," he said.

Ceff stepped inside, careful to keep his distance, and looked around the darkened room. He raised an eyebrow and I nodded.

"Jinx already left for the party," I said. "I was just..."

"Working up your courage?" he asked.

We hadn't been dating for very long, but Ceff knew me well. He was one of the few people I trusted enough to let my guard down with. I enjoyed being able to just be myself around Ceff. I smiled and gestured to the couch.

I sat at one end of the couch and turned on the table lamp. I knew that Ceff's eyes could see well enough in the dark, and my night vision was rapidly improving as my wisp abilities matured, but the darkness seemed too intimate. I sighed, folding my gloved hands in my lap, and perched on the edge of the couch. Jinx was right. I had issues.

"I have something for you," Ceff said.

He pulled a small, beribboned box from his pocket and set it on the couch between us. My Christmas present? But it wasn't Christmas yet.

I hesitated, hand shaking, as I leaned toward the package. Gifts made me nervous and the tiny box before me was no exception. But I didn't want to hurt Ceff's feelings. He looked so eager. I took a steadying breath and reached for the box.

I pulled the ribbon away and lifted the lid with the tips of my gloves. A seaweed covered item rested inside. Please say that wasn't jewelry, or a hat. Jinx would laugh for a week if she saw me wearing seaweed. Ceff cleared his throat and smiled.

"This was a boon from the selkie queen, the payment for my recent services to aid in the negotiations with her people," he said. Ceff's voice trickled over me like water, but I forced myself to pay attention to his words. "It grants the recipient one night without visions. She claimed that it was crafted with powerful magic at the request of a clairvoyant. How it came under the selkie queen's possession, I do not know."

Wait, a night without visions? But that meant...

"I could touch you," I said, a blush rising to burn my cheeks.

"Yes, but it is up to you how you wish to use it," he said.

He was saying that I didn't have to use the item to touch him, but Ceff looked pleased. I looked around the empty room. Jinx was at the party and would be dancing with Hans until dawn. I smiled a wicked grin, feeling giddy with excitement. Ceff had given me the best gift ever.

I reached for the magic seaweed and turned off the lamp.

CLUB NEXUS

AUTHOR'S NOTE

Club Nexus is comprised of four short stories—Iced, Dusted, Jinxed, and Demonized. I highly recommend reading these stories in order for the most powerful, and pleasurable, reading experience.

INTRODUCTION

Welcome to Club Nexus, a singular entertainment experience deep in the heart of Harborsmouth.

If you have discovered our exclusive club, then it's likely you belong to our specialized clientele. We cater to the needs and desires of vampires, demons, faeries, both Seelie and Unseelie, and their human servants.

To ensure the privacy of our patrons, a glamour has been cast to ward our club from detection by non-paranormals. We also provide club security, both at the door and within our fine establishment.

Our well-trained security staff do more than keep out unwelcome human riffraff. Due to our unique location atop crisscrossing ley lines, Club Nexus has been declared neutral ground. As such, we at Club Nexus have strict rules of conduct. Bloodshed must be consensual or the guilty parties risk punishment—death, maiming, or banishment from our club—at our security staff's discretion.

If you do hunger to satisfy unorthodox tastes and wish to walk the tightrope of our rules, you may be interested in the services of Mr. Goodfellow. Puck is a resourceful creature who will likely be able to provide what you desire—for a price.

We do hope you enjoy your visit to Club Nexus. Whether you are in need of a drink, a special someone, or a special someone to drink, we at Club Nexus are at your service.

ICED

I blew a stray lock of hair from my eyes while running a damp cloth over the bar. The raven black curl froze at the edge of my vision, ice crystals from my breath coating it like the dust of fractured diamonds. But within seconds the damp chunk of bangs thawed from the perpetual heat of the club.

The heat was one of the many things that I despised about bartending at Club Nexus. There were places within the club that were as cold as the Unseelie court I'd once called home—they had something here to please any fae in the upper echelons of power—but those areas were off limits to all but royalty and their trusted staff. Lowly club employees, such as myself, didn't make it past the velvet rope.

Not that a silly rope barrier would have kept me from the sweet embrace of one of the Winter Court's icy, private booths. No, the true deterrents were the heavily armed guards—a griffin with a razor sharp beak and a boggart with a particularly nasty disposition, even for one of my dark fae brethren. I sighed and pushed the lock of hair from my face, tucking it behind one of my pointy, blue ears.

I was proud of my pointy ears, slender figure, and unusual seven-foot height, for these things marked me as highborn fae. What I wasn't so keen on was my current living situation. Once upon a time, I'd graced the halls of the Winter Court in finery spun from spider silk, my hair pinned up with late blooming roses, strands of ice crystals around my neck. Now I was bedecked in an unflattering uniform, and had to bear drunken pickup lines from lowly light fae while serving my enemies drinks and cleaning up their messes. Oh, how the mighty had fallen.

I'd been tricked into an unfavorable bargain that left me with no alternative but to work off my debt here at Club Nexus as little more than a slave.

The man who'd tricked me, a notorious Seelie fae named Puck, was little more than a pimp. He used a number of underhanded methods to hold sway over a variety of races:

vamps, demons, humans, and fae. Puck ran girls through this
club for sex, blood, and sport. I suppose I should count myself
lucky that he'd been enamored by the idea of having an
Unseelie bartender who could chill drinks with her very breath,
but my position as a servant still rankled.

It was a predicament that should not have befallen one
of the highborn. I gripped the dishrag tight, the dirty remains
of spilled drinks dribbling down my wrist. I grimaced at the
foul liquid and tossed the rag into a bucket of soapy water.
Sulking wouldn't free me from this foul job, but an ear in the
right place just might.

I turned my attention to Puck, who had walked in
moments before and now had his head tilted close to the ear of
a vampire. They made an unlikely pair, the towheaded faerie
with his smiling cherubic face and the fanged vampire coated
in the dust of the grave. With the fangs of a vampire mere
inches from his jugular one might worry for Puck's safety, if
you didn't know who he really was.

No matter his appearance, Puck was no angel; his kind
was worse than any demon. He was a trickster who thrived on
chaos and the thrill of cheating others out of all they had,
whether that meant parting them from their money, their
blood, or their souls.

I moved toward the two on the pretense of feeding the
small faerie who provided illumination from within a glass
lantern further down the bar. I placed a scoop of honey inside
a trough cut into the base of the lantern and listened.

"In the market for a short or tall ten pints?" Puck asked.
"Had a new shipment of Ice in this week, so your drink can
come feisty or sedate. Take your pick."

My ears pricked at the mention of Ice—in the Winter
Court we had over three thousand words for ice—but I realized
that Puck was only discussing the drug he dealt to his special
clientele. The drug was used to subdue humans, and was
especially useful to vampires who wanted new blood slaves
without the bother of convincing the mortals fairly. Not that
seducing humans while using glamour to make themselves
irresistible would be considered fair to most mortals, but it was
a game we fae could understand. But the act of drugging their
victims senseless seemed like cheating.

I wrinkled my nose and turned away. I disliked vampires and the street names for what Puck was selling. "Ten pints" was slang for humans, since that was the quantity of blood in an average adult and "Ice" was the black market drug that numbed the minds of its users. The discussion of Puck's side business let me know that I'd learn nothing more of interest here. Puck was bargaining, not sharing damning secrets.

I needed to learn something I could use to gain my freedom, preferably a secret so dark that I could throw off my bonds and see the trickster bound into eternal suffering. Perhaps I'd find a way to make him my slave and let him lick my boots after a good wallow through yeti droppings. Information about drugs and blood slaves wasn't enough; I required something truly damning.

Arms hanging at my sides, I moved back to my post and sagged against the bar. Caught up in my own self-pity, I nearly missed the appearance of a woman who seemed to manifest on the stool in front of me. I reached for one of the pressed leaves we used for coasters and slid it onto the bar.

"What can I get you?" I asked.

I kept my eyes averted, studiously examining my cuticles. I'd found that it was easier to serve drinks when I didn't pay too much attention to the customers. You never know who might stroll through our doors. I would die of shame if one of my fellow highborn recognized me here in my servitude.

I waited for the woman's reply, but there was no answer. With a heavy sigh I glanced up to see the face that lay in shadow beneath the hood of a cloak of deep blue like the night sky. The cloak was beautiful, but the woman embraced within its folds was more remarkable still.

Ebony eyes stared from a face of pale, crystalline skin with lips the color of bruised inkberries. I knew that a kiss from those lips was just as poisonous as the bitter fruit they resembled.

"My l-l-l," I stuttered.

My liege, I'd meant to say, but the words were frozen on my tongue—literally. The woman seated before me was none other than Queen Mab, ruler of the Unseelie court. My queen had been absent these past hundred years and now here she was in Club Nexus, and she'd frozen my lips shut tight.

"Hush, my child," Mab said. "I am not yet ready for my whereabouts to become common knowledge. Our people have grown weak in my absence and I require your services to restore our court to its former glory. Will you assist your queen?"

I nodded, icy tears falling from my eyes to shatter on the hard surface of the bar.

"Good," she said. "I do believe you will enjoy the task I now set before you. Puck, Oberon's former lapdog, has been acquiring too much power in this city. Kill him quickly and quietly. I am granting you your freedom, Beryl. Do not waste this gift."

My heart swelled. Freedom at last! It was true that I'd sought a long, painful torment for the trickster, but if the Queen of Air and Darkness willed it, then I would kill Puck quickly.

"You will not remember our conversation, of course," she said. "My presence here in the mortal realms must not yet be revealed. But you are bound by our bargain all the same. Put down Oberon's pet and gain your freedom."

I blinked and rubbed my eyes, wondering why they were misted over and my cheeks were wet. Had I fallen asleep on the job? I glanced around quickly, hoping Puck hadn't noticed. The last time I dozed off while working, he'd held my hand over an open flame. The bastard knew of my aversion to fire and taunted me with it ceaselessly. Thankfully, Puck was too busy with his diversions to notice my lapse. He was only now leaving the dance floor with a curvaceous human on his arm.

I wiped absently at the counter in front of me, trying to look busy as I studied the trickster's new conquest. She bore multiple tattoos on her bare arms, but they didn't look like brandings or other marks of fae ownership. Examining her face, I could see that she was wearing heavy makeup, but her eyes were still bright and alert. The human wasn't on Ice, yet, but it wouldn't take Puck long if he wanted her dosed. All it would take was a quick sleight of hand while ordering her a drink and she'd be another slave to add to his larder.

I could have warned her. I'd done it more than once to thwart Puck's little games, but not tonight. I didn't care about the fate of this weak human. I had more important things to take care of, though I wasn't at all sure what those things were. For a moment, the room seemed to tilt on its axis and cool air whispered along my skin. I shook my head and continued wiping at the counter.

My hand hit a hard object and I looked down to see an ornate dagger in front of me. That was odd. I didn't remember any customers sitting here who may have left this behind. My eyes slid from the weapon to Puck striding this way. I grinned wide, seeing the chance I'd been looking for. I'd always dreamed of a long, slow revenge, but at the moment the thought of killing the trickster quickly and cleanly filled me with joy. Yes, he needed to be put down. Tonight.

As Puck walked past, I tossed my dishrag over the dagger and pulled it across the bar. Once he was gone, I slipped the blade into the pocket of my apron, the ice cold handle a comfort in my sweating hand. The weapon's sudden appearance must be a sign. I gripped the dagger tightly and slid into a nearby shadow.

My captor had gone through the door to the left of the bar and into the back storerooms. I knew what he did down below in the old wine cellars, and had learned to keep my distance from his special customers and their depravity.

But now I eyed the door with longing, wishing I had a way inside. Normally, I could make an excuse to run back for supplies, but it was a "special" night according to Puck and he'd locked the doors to all except paying guests.

One by one, vampires had been letting themselves in with newly crafted keys made of iron. I don't know how Puck managed to convey the keys to the vampires without suffering the effects of iron poisoning, but his security paid off. There was no way a faerie could steal one of those keys and gain admittance to his special bloodsucker party.

I was still glowering at the door when the southern vampire, who'd been sitting at the bar, stood and made his way toward the back room. As he slid a key from the pocket of his leather jacket, an idea sprung into my mind and I smiled. Heart racing, I grabbed a stack of bar towels, upended an unfinished drink on them, and hurried to his side.

"Excuse me," I said. "Can you hold the door? I need to swap these for clean linens or Puck will have my head."

A look of distaste crossed the vampire's face, either at such pushy behavior by a servant or the mention of Puck, I wasn't sure which. Maybe he was just annoyed that I'd delayed his dinner plans. Whatever the reason for his pinched expression, the vampire held the door while I scurried past, hurrying on once he'd followed me inside.

The vampire rushed past in a blur of movement, not willing to waste any more time before going below stairs. I shuddered, gripping the linens tight to my chest. The man probably already had his fangs in some poor schmuck's neck by now.

The door clicked shut and I released a shaky breath, setting the soiled towels on top of a low stack of cardboard boxes. The vampire hadn't bothered to switch on the lights in his hurried descent to the crypts below, and I certainly wasn't going to turn them on. The room was dark, but my Unseelie eyes were suited to lurking in shadows and I didn't want to alert Puck, or any of the vampires being entertained with blood and vice, to my presence.

I tiptoed to the door we'd just come through and, after placing my ear to the wood to listen for anyone approaching, bent low and blew an icy mist into the lock. When the keyhole was filled with ice, I turned toward the stairs at the back of the room.

Silently, I dodged crates and boxes, making my way across the room and down a flight of stairs. At the bottom, I could hear movement and the dry, hacking sound of a laughing vampire. Beneath it all ran a soundtrack of agony: moans, cries, and shrieks of pain or terror. I swallowed hard and pulled myself up to my full seven-foot height.

Soon I would be free of this prison and though the roads to the Winter Court were sealed, I'd find a new place to live where the ones crying out in agony were Seelie fae, as it should be. I imagined Puck chained in iron and strung from one of the court's elaborately carved balconies. How Mab would have laughed at such a sight. She always did love the sweet taste of revenge.

I blinked back icy tears at the memory of my lost queen—if only she'd return to us!—and pulled the dagger from my apron. Strangely, the weapon made me feel closer to my liege.

I moved forward, but as I was about to turn the corner into the wine cellar, I heard the faint scuff of a boot on the stairs. I ducked into deeper darkness behind a rack of wine bottles, embracing the shadows as I held my breath.

Seconds later, a man in an old-fashioned waistcoat came into view. I frowned, studying the man as he descended the stairs. How had he opened the locked door above? The ice I'd frozen the lock shut with shouldn't have melted so quickly.

Flame flickered in the man's eyes, providing my answer. The dapper gentleman was a demon.

After surveying the room and tugging at his gloves, the demon continued on. I listened, wondering if I should make my escape before more partygoers made their way through the door and down the stairs. I dug my fingernails into my palm, trying to stem the wave of dizziness that threatened to overwhelm me. If I was discovered, Puck would take great pleasure in my punishment.

The sound of an argument and Puck's strained voice convinced me to stay. For once, the trickster sounded worried. Plus, I couldn't shake the feeling that I had a duty to fulfill.

I pressed my lips together and crept out from behind the racks of wine, inching my way along the demon's trail. At the first open doorway, I could hear the demon and Puck arguing. I stole a glance into the room, and jerked my head back.

A slow smile spread across my face, the upturned curve of my lips feeling odd after so many years of enslavement. The demon was circling Puck, keeping him distracted and off balance. I had no idea what their argument was about— money, a girl, a drug deal gone wrong—and I didn't care. What I saw in that room was an opportunity.

I slipped a hand into my apron, gripping the jeweled dagger. This was my chance.

With a wild yell and bark of laughter, I rushed into the room. I raised my arm, thrusting the dagger toward Puck's heart—if the bastard even had one—but was wrenched to the side as a vampire appeared before me.

The southern vamp from the bar, I thought as my vision tunneled, shadows racing in from the periphery. I tried to move again toward Puck, but pain slammed into me. I gagged and slid to my knees.

The vampire snarled, holding a bloody, lifeless arm in his grasp. Confused, I looked down to see my own arm missing, blood oozing from my shoulder. Understanding dawned and I smiled. I'd be out from under Puck's thumb no matter what happened now.

I fumbled at my apron with the fingers of my remaining hand, muscles already growing slow and weak. The demon continued his argument with Puck and the vampire was babbling about the need to protect Bite Club or some such nonsense. My head buzzed and my vision blurred.

I didn't have much time.

I extracted the ice pick from the torn seam where I'd kept it, longing for the day I'd win my freedom. It wasn't as elegant as the jeweled dagger, but it would have to do.

I managed to get a foot under me and lunged, jamming the ice pick upward. I felt the silver punch through muscle and slip beneath the ribs and into Puck's heart. His eyes widened in surprise and I laughed.

Adrenaline fading, I hung limply in the arms of the vampire who'd grabbed hold of me. Licking my lips, I looked up into the frenzied face of the vampire. The creature latched onto my neck, sinking his fangs into my jugular, but I no longer cared.

"I did as you asked, my queen," I rasped.

My vision dimmed to a tiny point of light and my body felt pleasantly cold. I relaxed, a smile still on my lips. I'd served my queen and been granted my own wish. No more tending bar in a sweaty nightclub. No further decades of servitude to the almighty Puck, who was now dying alongside me in this moldering, old wine cellar.

I was free.

DUSTED

The first rule of Bite Club is *there are no rules.* The lack of restrictions is what makes our soirees so dang irresistible. Bite Club is an all you can eat buffet of blood and wanton pleasure. But like all good things, Bite Club comes in small doses.

If vampires bit and drained everything in sight on a regular basis, we'd be hunted, staked, and burned to ash never to rise again. I tugged at the brim of my hat, which sat catawampus from a burst of speed, and made my way down the spiral staircase toward the bar.

I'm not a rogue—I can play by the rules—but immortality is a long, long lifetime and I'd found that Bite Club helped its members cope with the boredom and frustrations of eternal life beneath Vampire Law.

The vampire council mandates that all new fledglings adhere to their laws, or perish. What our masters don't bother to tell us is that even after decades of following the rules to the letter, the restrictions do not lift. And after half a century, the laws regarding how one must conduct a hunt had begun to chafe.

Vampire Law states that feeding must be done discreetly. Blood slaves, humans who give their blood willingly, are encouraged—so long as we only make slaves of those unfortunate souls whom human society has already forsaken. We feed off the fringe of humanity—the homeless, addicts, runaways—those who are unlikely to be missed or whose disappearance can easily be explained away. But this forced discretion scraped against my true nature like a wooden stake against my heart. Vampires are predators, not scavenging birds meant to swoop in and pick at the garbage that humans cast aside.

I am no trash pickin' gull. I am a vampire.

When I was first turned, I left the familiar bayous of my hometown seeking freedom. I had hoped that a change of scenery and putting distance between me and my master would alleviate the feeling of suffocation that plagued my new existence. Who would have known the undead led such a repressed life after death?

Inching my way north, I'd found my salvation in a dockside tavern outside Boston. I'd met a man, much like this Puck I was to meet with tonight, who organized a special club for vampires who wanted a taste of excitement—and blood.

I was indoctrinated into Bite Club, a no fangs barred gathering of vampires who, like me, chafed at the rules that bound our daily lives. At one of our meetings, humans could be purchased and, so long as we were within the confines of the designated location, we could do what we wanted with them. Some meetings were in places suitable for hunting games while others were in more comfortable settings for sating hunger for something other than blood.

But no matter what, the venue had always changed. That was why I got so excited when I learned of this place. Following rumors from other members, I was led to a city where Bite Club was hosted not once, but many times at a place called Club Nexus. The meetings were behind closed doors, down in the club's wine cellars, but I didn't mind the crypt-like setting if it meant I could have my fun without interruption. Puck made sure that only well-vetted members were allowed admittance, so there was no risk of punishment from the Vampire Council.

I smiled, the skin stretching tight across the bones of my face. It wasn't breaking the law if the uppity council didn't know about it.

I sidled up to the bar, awed once again by the shelves of glowing liquids encased in glass bottles. None of these victuals would sustain me, there was only one substance now that could accomplish that, but I ordered a shot of bourbon anyway. I stared into my glass, watching the blue, green, and pink reflections sparkle across the surface, while I waited for my contact to arrive.

I breathed deeply as two women, one fae and one human, crossed the room heading toward the other end of the bar. I no longer had to breathe to survive, but I scented their blood like a sommelier running wine along the tongue. The faerie smelled like toasted pain and simmering hope, as if she was a creature of fire who'd long been broken and was only now beginning to put the pieces of her life back together. The human lacked the subtleties of fae scent, but her blood pounded tantalizingly beneath the skin and her hair smelled like cherry blossoms.

As a fool boy, I'd picked bushels of cherries from a nearby orchard and ate until I thought I would burst. Groaning with an upset stomach from overeating, I'd felt dumber than a stump, that was certain, but now I'd give anything for that sated feeling. I needed an abundance of blood and pain to feel content these days, both of which were in short supply while following the rules of Vampire Law.

I flicked my eyes to the shifting purple sand in the hourglass suspended above the bar. Puck was late.

I didn't care for Puck's company; he was slicker than a bullfrog in a rainstorm. But I had to admit, for a faerie, he was sensible. He'd had the horse sense to make a regular business of the Bite Club clientele and our sundry needs. Deviance is nothing if not full of variety and Puck had discovered how to capitalize on each and every one of our desires. In fact, I wouldn't be surprised if the imp was purposely late to our meetings to build the suspense, and empty my wallet.

I scowled at the time and massaged my temples. *Where the devil was he?* Beneath my glamour, my fangs lengthened. I needed to feed, now. Perhaps if I bought the ladies at the other end of the bar a drink, I could lure them into a shadowy corner. The council be damned.

I was so caught up in the dust storm of my thoughts that I jumped when a hand slapped my back. I turned to see the body of a young man attached to the offending hand. Puck appeared to be about seventeen, no more than three years younger than I'd been when I was turned, but his dimples and mop of curly, blond hair gave his face a childish innocence. As my ma would have said, he was cuter than a box of puppies.

And like a puppy, he'd be happy to take all I had to give and then shit in my boots. Too bad he was the only purveyor of vice—true vice, the kind without limits—in this god forsaken town.

"You're late," I said. I tossed back the bourbon and upended the empty glass, slamming it on the bar with a wallop.

"Sorry, Cyrus," Puck said. The curl of his lip was enough to know the faerie's apology wasn't genuine, but I held myself rigid. Tearing off this one's head would do me no good. More's the pity.

"I ain't seen hide nor hair of you all evenin'," I said. I frowned around my fangs, trying to ignore the ache in my jaw.

"Busy night," Puck said with a shrug.

Puck looked around the bar and smiled at one of the women I'd been stalking. *My prey.* The predator in me wanted to lash out and tear his spine through his eye socket, but I pressed my lips together and remained seated on the barstool. The faerie may be too big for his britches, but he'd provide me with a dinner date soon enough.

"Got what I came for?" I asked. No sense in waiting while Puck made eyes at the human woman. I was past waiting on the man. It was time to get down to business.

"In the market for a short or tall ten pints?" he asked. "Had a new shipment of Ice in this week, so your drink can come feisty or sedate. Take your pick."

Ice was the drug Puck was peddling lately. I reckoned it was some magic concoction that gave paranormals a euphoric high and left humans stoned out of their right minds.

"I prefer my meal kickin' and screamin'," I said.

I couldn't abide my prey drugged six ways to Sunday. Where was the fun in that?

"Feisty it is then," he said.

"When can I eat?" I asked.

"In good time," he said. "Like I said, it's been a busy night and you're not the only vampire in this city with needs."

"I shouldn't oughta have to wait," I said.

"Don't worry, my friend," he said. "You won't have to wait much longer. Customer in front of you is a quick feeder. Man will be done in fifteen minutes tops. Give him time to finish up."

"Fine," I said, holding out my hand.

Puck upended a velvet bag embroidered with arcane symbols and handed over an iron key.

"At my signal, enter the basement—no sooner," he said. "Use the room on the right, same as last time. Your toys are already laid out for you."

I fidgeted on my stool and tried not to gaze longingly at the basement door. As soon as the vampire ahead of me was done feeding, it'd just be me, my prey, and a room full of chains. I'd be happier than a pig in poop.

Puck stood and slapped me on the back.

"Gotta run, Cyrus," he said. "Have fun."

"Always do," I said.

I spoke into empty space. The faerie was already strutting down the bar toward the human woman and her friend. I turned back to the hourglass and clicked my fingernails against the bar top. It seemed like ages for the other vampire to clear out of the basement, but finally, a vampire who looked like some Yankee Wall Street stock broker came out of the door in a blur.

It's hard to keep our otherness in check immediately after a feed. The blood games provide a euphoric rush that pushes our bodies to glory in our vampiric speed and strength. The Yankee vampire held his body at odd angles, cracked the back of a chair he touched in passing, and moved too quickly. Evidently, he'd drunk his fill.

So where in the Hell was Puck?

I focused on the faerie's voice and soon pinpointed his location. He hadn't gone far. He was with the human woman and her intoxicated friend. Judging from Puck's face, his attempts to win over the two women hadn't gone well. If I wasn't so hungry, the thought would have made me smile. Instead, I grimaced, waiting for Puck to get on with it.

Finally, after an eternity spent spying on Puck's flirtations with the human woman, he came walking my way. As he passed the bar, Puck reached up to scratch at his cheek with two fingers. That was the signal; *two minutes.*

From the corner of my eye, I watched Puck saunter over toward a table of vampires at the edge of the dance floor. He passed something to one of the men and continued on toward the basement door at the end of the bar.

A pulse of pleasure raced up my spine and my fangs tingled with anticipation. I'd exercised enough patience and restraint for one night. I'd sat like a bump on a log while that other vampire drank his fill.

Now it was my turn.

I slid liquidly from the barstool and turned away from the crowd. Patting the key in my front pocket, I walked down the bar toward the basement door.

A woman brushed by, the edges of her midnight blue cloak twining around my ankles like coldblooded serpents. I shivered, which was something I hadn't done since my human days. The cold doesn't generally affect you once you've felt the chill of the grave. My reaction was odd enough to make me turn around, seeking the mysterious woman. But the cloaked figure was gone.

I clenched my jaw in frustration, and my thirst returned. A woman that beautiful was as scarce as hen's teeth, but I wasn't interested enough to attempt pursuit. There wasn't much that could distract me when I'd set my mind to the pleasures of a blood hunt. The creatures who frequented this club may allow a taste, but often for a hefty price, and they'd never let me play the games I truly desired.

My head snapped back to focus on the door just to the left of the bar. Behind that door lay what I sought. *Your toys are already laid out for you.* I felt a slow smile skitter across my face. I had a good feeling about tonight.

Boots whispering along the floor, I pulled the key from my pocket and forced myself to walk, not run, to the door. Desire stirred within me like cream in a butter churn. Beyond that unassuming portal lay a world of pleasures.

"Excuse me," said a voice at my shoulder. I scowled and pulled my gaze from the door. I'd been waylaid by the blue-skinned bartender. I recognized her as the one who'd poured my glass of bourbon. "Can you hold the door? I need to swap these for clean linens or Puck will have my head."

Puck might "have her head" for slacking in her duties, but the woman had no idea how close I was to literally tearing her head from her body and tossing it across the room like a hot tater. Too bad that kind of ruckus would draw the attention of club security, and put a kink in my plans.

"Fine," I said, opening the door. "Now go on and quit piddlin', or I'll leave you out here."

The faerie woman scurried inside, arms laden with soiled linens. Once inside, for just a moment, I considered taking the bartender as an appetizer, but then I heard a cry from below. Puck was tenderizing my meal. Time to get a move on.

Casks of wine moved by in a blur of motion as I nearly flew through the storeroom and down a flight of stairs, leaving the faerie woman behind. I continued on, slipping through the shadows without the need of a light, following the sound of someone pitchin' a hissy fit.

They always did that when the Ice wore off. Don't know how Puck managed to time it so perfectly. I reckon he drugged them at a specified time, making our meals suggestible and easy to transport into the basement rooms where we had our fun. Of course, we predators prefer our meals feisty. It wouldn't do to have our prey ruffied to Hell and gone. What'd be the fun in that?

I pulled up short to see Puck in the doorway to my usual room.

"I've outdone myself with this one, Cyrus," Puck said, gesturing for me to look inside the room.

For once, the faerie was giving it to me straight. The woman shackled to the wall was finer than frog's hair. Like a human's palate, vampires have preferences for what's on the menu, and this woman was just my type.

"She's a spittin' image," I said.

I'd given Puck a faded photograph to go by and tonight he'd come through in spades. The auburn-haired beauty was struggling against the manacles and nekked as a jaybird. My fangs lengthened and an ache coursed through my body.

I reached into my coat and tossed an envelope of cash toward the retreating faerie. I closed the door, knowing Puck wouldn't go far. No matter what the man claimed about running this business for profit, he was in it for more than the money.

On more than one occasion the faerie had lingered outside the door of my room while I fed. Judging from the pheromones coming off the guy, Puck liked to listen. Well goody for him, tonight he was in for a treat.

I set to work on the woman, calling her by the name of someone long dead and gone. I tried to make it last, savor the aroma of her fear, but she reminded me so much of an irretrievable past. Within seconds she was bleeding like a stuck pig. I fed quickly and deeply, pausing only when I heard a ruckus outside the door.

Someone had entered the basement and was arguing with Puck. Best see what all the fuss was about. I may not like the man, but Puck provided me with warm meals like this one. I pulled an arm across my mouth and went to listen at the door.

"Playing at judge, jury, and executioner?" Puck asked. "That's not like you, Forneus. Heck, I didn't think you had the balls. Good for you."

I swung the door open, nearly taking it from its hinges, and ran to defend Puck. A demon stood facing Puck from across the room and the blue-skinned bartender was rushing toward Puck with her arm raised, a jeweled dagger in her hand.

"No one threatens Bite Club," I snarled.

I slid in front of Puck and hissed, spittle and blood flecking the wide-eyed faerie woman. In the same motion, I planted my feet wide, grabbed the woman's arm and wrenched it free from her body. The jeweled dagger that'd been plunging toward Puck's chest was no longer a threat.

I flung the arm across the room, nostrils flaring and fangs aching. Even full as a tick from my previous meal, the blood spraying from the faerie's shoulder held my rapt attention. A coil of need grew inside my gut.

Once again, it was time to feed.

The faerie lunged toward Puck, and I struck. I latched onto her neck, sinking my fangs in deep and letting the rapid pulse of the artery carry me away.

Lost in a sea of blood dreams, I lost track of events. But as the faerie's heart faltered, I came to my senses and scanned the room for additional threats.

Flame flickered along the demon's fingers, making me flinch, and a human woman came rushing into the room, crossbow at the ready. At first, the human aimed the bow at the demon and I thought she'd take care of the man for me. But she spun and trained her bow on me, demanding I release the faerie girl.

I tossed the corpse to the ground. I no longer needed the faerie woman; she was drier than a bar on Sunday. But the human was another story.

I rushed forward, the sting of a crossbow bolt not even making me pause. The bolt wasn't wood, so it couldn't stop me, but I'd still make the woman pay for the minor wound. My fingernails lengthened as I extended my hands toward the woman—all the better to flay the flesh from her bones.

I reached out, closing the distance, but suddenly the woman was gone and the demon was standing in front of me. Before I had time to wonder where my prey had gone, a blinding pain shot through my chest. Then all I could see was the ceiling.

I'd been staked.

I tried to move, but I was weak as a lamb. I couldn't so much as flex my fingers. I strained to hear past the ringing in my ears, wondering what the demon had planned for the likes of me. Probably nothing good.

I reckoned I was past redemption now. I'd broken Vampire Law and was beyond receiving help from the council. Puck lay bleeding close by, not that he was even a friend. For the first time in decades, I felt remorse. How long had it been since I'd had faithful friends or allies to watch my back?

My past was steeped in blood. After my rising, I'd killed everyone who'd ever mattered to me as a human. I'd murdered my friends and family and reveled in their pain.

Eventually, the demon came to stand over me, flame flickering in his eyes. I knew then what he meant to do and, surprisingly, a part of me welcomed this final judgment. All things have an ending, and I'd had a long unlife.

I'd cheated death and caused a speedbump in the cycle of life. I should have died long ago. When the flames came, I smiled. It was time to complete the cycle.

It was time to return to dust.

JINXED

Of all the nightclubs, in all the cities, in all the world,
the freakin' demon had to walk into Club Nexus. My nickname,
Jinx, had never seemed more appropriate. I really was one of
the unluckiest people on the planet.

The sight of Forneus striding purposefully across the
club toward me made my breath quicken and skin tingle. I
tried to look away, or at least stammer a warning to Ivy who
was ordering our drinks, but my body had gone on strike,
completely disconnecting from my brain. Anger and desire
stole the words from my lips and I continued to face the demon
head on.

When it came to Forneus, I admit, I have issues.

I desperately wanted to kiss the man and shoot him in
equal parts. That's the problem with the demon lawyer. He is
so frustratingly attractive and yet every time he opens his
mouth I feel the urge to wipe that smug smile off his face—with
a sledgehammer. Every move of his powerful body, every
gesture of his slender hands, and every leer down his aquiline
nose sent waves of heat down into my belly and made my blood
boil.

Yes, I should definitely shoot him.

Since Forneus was a demon, he'd probably survive the
shooting, might even enjoy it if I hadn't dipped my crossbow
bolts in holy water before leaving the loft. I slipped my hand
from the bar and reached over my shoulder to where my
crossbow was slung, keeping my eyes on the demon. My
fingers traced the handle of the weapon and I licked my lips in
anticipation.

Forneus approached from the side opposite Ivy and slid
an arm around my waist. Warmth spread through me and
need spiraled low in my belly. As if sensing my desire, a
knowing smile lifted his lips and heat simmered in his eyes.

I shifted in my seat, giving Forneus a leer of my own,
and froze. Ivy, glowing wildly like a fourth of July sparkler,

was there in a flash, holding a knife to Forneus' throat. Damn, she was fast—and pissed.

Even if her glowing skin hadn't given away my friend's agitation, then the sheen of sweat on her upper lip and her rapid breathing would have been a clear indication of just how much Ivy loathed the idea of coming this close to touching an immortal demon. Well, when it came to this particular demon that was something we both had in common.

And it wasn't demon cooties she was worried about. If so much as an inch of her skin brushed against Forneus, Ivy would be trapped in millennia of nightmare visions, direct from Hell. And that was one station I'm sure she didn't want to tune into, ever. But here she was, holding one of her blades to his throat. Her gloved hand barely shook as she stared down the demon.

It was then that I realized the music had stopped. In fact, the entire club had gone silent as a grave, every single breathing patron holding their collective breath. I flicked my eyes around to see hundreds of faeries, and even a few vamps, staring at Ivy's blade where it dug into Forneus' throat. The only movement was from a half dozen large ogres as they pushed their way through the crowd.

Heart racing like the dance music that should have been playing, my hand tightened on the crossbow, and I thumbed off the safety. Had it been foolish to cock and load the bow before entering the club? Probably, but I was now happy that I had. If the club's bouncers turned on me and Ivy, we'd go down fighting.

A growling voice, preceded by a quick puff of air, warned me of a newcomer to the fight. I sucked in a shaky breath and turned to see a griffin alight on top of the barstool Ivy had vacated.

"I wouldn't do that if I were you, human," he said.

The dog-sized creature had arrived before the other bouncers by using its wings to fly over the crowded room. Though smaller than the fast approaching ogres, the griffin looked just as deadly. An eagle head sporting a hooked beak rested atop the body of a lion, claws and all.

"Why not?" I asked, keeping my voice low. "What's going on?"

"You've threatened violence within the club's walls," the griffin said. "There will be no bloodshed here. Club Nexus is neutral ground. If you wish to kill each other, take it outside."

"This is all a misunderstanding," Forneus said, spreading his hands wide. "These lovely ladies weren't threatening me, Gregor, not against my will. This was just a little game we concocted. To keep things...interesting."

"Demons," the griffin spat under his breath.

"What?" Forneus asked, eyes wide. "Eternity is a long time, as you well know. A man must do something to spice things up a bit now and again."

The griffin, Gregor, frowned, but nodded to the ogres who now stood at Ivy's back. One of the ogres cracked his knuckles, but none of them reached for my friend. I took that as a good sign. Especially since one of those hands could palm Ivy's head like a softball.

"You know the rules, Forneus," Gregor said. "If your games involve consensual violence, you must submit the appropriate paperwork to club security. Nearly any behavior is allowed with a proper permit, but we do not allow anarchy within these walls."

"Paperwork," Forneus muttered, rolling his eyes. "You're all nearly as bad as Hell."

"In the meantime," Gregor said, turning to Ivy. "Sheath your weapons. There will be no bloodshed without filing the necessary paperwork."

The demon sighed and folded his arms across his chest.

"Might as well do as they say, darling," he said. "You can't cut through this red tape with weapons. But if you do decide to fight, I'm happy to provide you with legal services...for a nominal fee."

I shook my head at the demon lawyer's offer. Pay Forneus to get us out of this jam? Over my dead body. As I saw it, it was his fault we were in trouble with club security in the first place. I snorted and inched away from the demon. At least his arm was no longer wrapped around my waist.

Ivy looked at me and I nodded, slipping an empty hand into my lap. Cutting Forneus' throat and impaling him with a crossbow bolt were things that would just have to wait. Ivy lowered her blade and shoved it into a sheath concealed beneath her leather jacket. In one quick movement, she slid away from Forneus and leaned against the bar at my side.

"Are we good, griffin?" she asked, never taking her eyes off Forneus.

"Yes, Princess," Gregor said. "Do try to follow the rules in the future."

Ivy grunted an affirmative and the griffin took wing. Apparently, that was the signal for the club to return to normal. Music pulsed through the room and dancers returned to their earlier swaying and gyrating.

Scowling, Ivy slid back onto her bar stool and turned to watch demon.

"Ah, now, where were we?" Forneus asked. He moved closer, brushing against my leg. "Shall I buy you that drink?"

Forneus perched on the edge of the barstool beside me and now that we weren't being chewed out by club security, I couldn't help but notice that he smelled different. Was that cologne...and mouthwash? Was Forneus trying to cover up the stench of brimstone that usually clung to him like a hellspawn fart? Whatever he'd done, it was an improvement. Heat flared from where our legs touched and I wondered if he tasted as good as he smelled...

Forneus turned a raised eyebrow my way, but I was so distracted that I'd forgotten the question. I blushed, trying to remember what he'd asked. Ivy bristled at my side, her skin glowing so brightly that I had to blink rapidly to keep my eyes from tearing up.

"Um..." I said.

"No," Ivy said.

I shook my head, clearing away the ridiculous impulse to crawl into Forneus' lap and run my hands through his slicked back hair. Right, the demon had offered to buy me a drink. *Get a grip, Jinx.* Geesh, I was here to celebrate the end of my relationship with Hans. I wasn't here to hook up with some new guy worthy of a stabbing.

"No thanks, Forneus," I said. "I'd rather chew on thumbtacks."

"Really?" he asked, eyelids at half-mast. Those bedroom eyes nearly did me in, but Ivy slid off her stool, hands twitching at her sides. I knew that with her new faerie speed, she could have a blade at Forneus' throat again in a second, and to hell with the consequences. "Fine, fine. Until later, ladies."

With a wink and a bow, Forneus turned and slipped away into the crowd, leaving an empty ache in my gut. I put a hand to my stomach, wishing my traitorous feelings would stop complicating my life. Having the hots for a sexy demon was not a problem I needed right now.

"I don't know what you see in him," Ivy said.

"What do you mean?" I asked.

"Are you telling me you didn't just stare at his butt like it was a double-fudge brownie?" she asked, raising her eyebrows.

I shrugged and turned back to the bar.

"You two need to figure things out soon, before someone gets killed in the crossfire," she said.

"Figure what out?" I asked, staring at the colorful, glowing bottles that lined the shelves behind the bar.

"Like if you want to throw the guy into bed or an empty grave," she said.

I sighed and picked at a drink coaster, crumpling bits of confetti onto the ebony bar. At least, I thought it was a coaster. Up close it resembled a dried out leaf. Weirdo faeries.

"I guess I want a bit of both," I said, turning to Ivy. She groaned and squeezed her eyes shut. "What?"

"Just had an image of you humping the demon lawyer in a graveyard," she said.

"Yeah, me too," I said with a sigh. I let my head drop into my hands, elbows resting on the leaf-strewn bar. "I can't decide if I need brain bleach or a crate of condoms. Heck, do demons have STDs?"

"Mab's bones, I don't want to know," she said, wrinkling her nose. "I don't even know how you can stand the stench."

"You mean his cologne?" I asked. I thought he smelled...yummy.

"Is that what we're calling it now?" she asked. "He smells like hellfire and brimstone. It makes my sinuses burn."

"That's weird," I said. "I've smelled that on him in the past, but tonight I thought he smelled good. Like he'd put on cologne and swished with some kind of cinnamon mouthwash or like he'd been sucking on hot balls. No demon stench at all."

"You did not just say his breath, a demon's breath, smelled like hot balls," she said. Ivy slapped a gloved hand over her mouth, but her eyes were laughing at me.

"And I can't believe you just went there," I said, chuckling. "Who are you and what have you done with my prudish friend? Which reminds me, we still haven't talked about you and Ceff. I want to hear all about the hot kelpie sex."

Ivy sighed.

"I think we need those drinks," she said.

Our drinks still sat on the bar where Ivy had left them before the Forneus drama. She slid a pint glass toward me and raised her own in mock salute. I noticed that Ivy's had a familiar chip in the side and wondered how she'd talked the bartender into serving her in her own glass. Who knows, maybe weird requests like that weren't that unusual around here. They did use dead tree droppings as coasters.

"To girls' night out," I said, smiling.

"May we survive it," she replied. Ivy knocked back her drink and wiped her sleeve across her mouth. "So, can we go home now?"

"No way," I said. "I'm not going anywhere until I dance with at least one decent guy."

"I was afraid of that," she said.

Ivy's eyes continued to scan the room, always on the alert for threats. I followed her gaze, sizing up each eligible bachelor in the place. In a club this huge, you'd think there would be plenty of available hotties, but a quick survey of the dance floor only made me want to go home and hug my crossbow.

"There's got to be one man here who doesn't want to eat my face or plant mutant babies in my eyeballs," I said.

Ivy chuckled and shook her head. I was exaggerating, a bit, but there were some pretty freaky fae creatures here. For every beautiful faerie, there was something that looked like a monster from Saturday morning cartoons. And though vamps looked yummy enough to my eyes—the faerie ointment I wore didn't cut through undead glamour—Ivy had assured me that I didn't want to date one. No matter how sexy their glamour made them look, embracing bones, fangs, and corpse dust was just not my thing.

"What about him?" Ivy asked, studying a guy who was standing further down the bar. "He looks harmless, for a faerie, and he's kinda cute."

I took in the boyish face and shock of curly, blond hair and sighed. He was cute, but not really my type. He was above average height and covered in lean muscle, but his golden curls would have suited one of those creepy, naked babies they put on Valentine's Day cards and his skin looked softer than mine.

"I prefer mature men," I said. "He's probably jailbait."

Ivy laughed.

"I doubt it," she said. "He's probably hundreds of years older than you."

He turned our way and smiled and I nearly rolled my eyes. The guy even had dimples. Ivy waved and I resisted the urge to punch her. Jailbait was now walking our way.

"Great, look what you've done," I whispered. "Since he's on his way over, can you at least tell if he's Seelie or Unseelie fae?"

Not that a faerie's court affiliation meant they were necessarily good or evil. Ivy was half wisp and Ceff was a kelpie, both of the Unseelie court, and they didn't act like they had gone over to the dark side. But I figured it was best to be forewarned. I just wished faeries walked around with different colored lightsabers or something so I could tell which team they were on.

"I'm a light fae," the guy said, stepping up to my side. "And you must be the lovely human everyone is whispering about tonight."

Crap. Pesky faerie hearing. I should have learned by now that the tricksy immortals could hear from across the room, if they wanted to. Leave it to me to open my mouth and insert a pair of platform sandals.

"Um, good to know you're one of the good guys," I said. "I'm Jinx."

"Puck," he said, reaching for and kissing the back of my hand. His green eyes twinkled and that dimple was back, but Ivy was right. There was something about him that seemed older than his apparent eighteen or so years.

"As in THE Puck?" Ivy asked.

I pulled my hand back, thankful for the interruption. For a moment, I'd felt like Puck and I were standing alone in an ancient forest. I wiped my hand down my thigh, wondering if the lingering scent of pine and sound of dead, rustling leaves was only my imagination. Had this innocent looking guy worked some kind of faerie magic on me? And if kissing my hand had sent us into some dreamy forest, what would a real kiss do? A shiver ran along my spine; I wasn't sure if I wanted to find out.

"The one and only," he said. He leaned in so close that I could count the freckles that dotted his nose and cheeks. "Have you heard of me?"

He waggled his eyebrows and Ivy laughed, but I just sat there, wishing I'd ordered a second drink. I knew my brain was scrambled after the encounter with Forneus, but I had no idea what they were talking about. I was pretty sure I'd never heard the name Puck in my life.

"No, are you famous or something?" I asked.

"More like notorious," Ivy said, smiling. "Puck here made it into Shakespeare's play *A Midsummer Night's Dream.* If the Bard is to be believed, he's something of a trickster."

Ivy's mom had been big into Shakespeare, which explained how my friend had heard of Puck. I liked old books, music, and movies, but my idea of retro was the early 1900's, not the dinosaur age.

"Thou speak'st aright; I am that merry wanderer of the night," he said with a bow.

So this guy Puck was some kind of celebrity faerie trickster? What, exactly, did that mean?

"So, um, what kind of tricks are we talking about?" I asked. "Nair in shampoo bottles? Sticking firecrackers up a frog's butt?"

Oops. I felt heat rise to my face, wishing again for that second drink. I swear sometimes my mouth has a mind of its own. Thankfully, Puck smiled and laughed like what I'd said was meant to be funny.

"Nothing that bad," he said. "Just kid stuff. Plus, that was the old Puck. I'm a reformed sinner."

"What made you change your ways?" I asked.

Crap, it sounded like I was flirting, but I was actually curious. In my experience, guys didn't change much, even when they wanted you to think they would. How many times had I heard, "I'll stop cheating, I promise" from one of my exes? But maybe when a guy lived for centuries there was room for change—maybe being the operative word.

"Everything changed after Oberon left court," he said, face darkening. His gaze seemed to turn inward for a moment until he shook his head and shrugged. "But that's ancient history."

I *had* heard of Oberon, the king of the Seelie court, and how the king and queens of Faerie had disappeared from their courts hundreds of years ago, but I didn't have time to consider Puck's comment. A new song started and Ivy gave me an encouraging thumbs-up sign from over Puck's shoulder. I rolled my eyes and looked around for Forneus. Not that I really cared what he was doing or anything. I was just curious, that's all.

"Oh, wow, Jinx loves this song," she said. "Don't you Jinx?"

I nodded wondering what Ivy was playing at, since I'd never heard music like this in my entire life. Puck scraped a hand through his flyaway curls and flashed a smile from beneath long lashes.

"Care to dance?" he asked.

The faerie held out his hand and I hesitated. I'd wanted to dance, but Puck wasn't really my type. I looked around, trying to think of an excuse to put him off, when my eyes fell on Forneus. He hadn't gone far and was now watching me and Puck with a frown marring his lips. On impulse, I grabbed Puck's hand and slid from the barstool.

"I'd love to," I said. "Ivy, you'll be okay here?"

I dropped my crossbow onto the barstool I'd just vacated, since I didn't plan to shoot anyone on the dance floor. I might as well leave Ivy with the extra arsenal, just in case.

"I'll be fine," she said, waving me off. "Go, have fun."

I pulled Puck toward the dance floor, letting my hips sway as I sashayed away from the bar and Forneus, just in case the demon was still watching. I glanced over my shoulder to smile at Puck and could have sworn his face held the sly, hungry look of a fox in a henhouse. But strobe lights flashed on and off and the look was gone as if I'd imagined it. I probably had. Obsessing over Forneus was making me crazy.

Even preoccupied with demon watching, I couldn't help but notice that Puck was a popular guy. Male and female faeries flirted as we waded through their intricate dances and more than one vamp whispered something about ice. Maybe Puck worked here tending bar or waiting tables? If so, he was obviously off duty and gave each vamp the brush off, mentioning something about pleasure before business. It didn't take him long to get down to his idea of pleasure on the dance floor.

"So, Jinx," Puck said, pressing close. "Is that your True Name?"

He stroked the inside of my palm in slow circles with his thumb and I dropped his hand to adjust my dress—without much success. It was like trying to toss away a booger tissue; the damn thing just wouldn't let go.

Puck mashed himself between my hips, swaying to the music and pulling me along with him. He cupped my ass with sweaty hands and pulled me close enough to know he was interested in more than dancing. I figured we were giving Forneus quite the show, which had been my intent, but now that we were on the dance floor, I felt the urge to flee.

I couldn't quite put my finger on it, but there was something about Puck that set off my internal bullshit meter. I just wasn't buying his harmless kid act, and I was pretty sure his groping wasn't due to inexperience. With the bruises from Hans' temper still visible every damn time I washed off my makeup, I was on high alert for abusive asshole warning signs. And Puck squeezing my ass? Yeah, he was making me wish I'd brought my crossbow onto the dance floor after all.

"No, but all my friends call me Jinx," I said.

I tried to force a smile and bat my eyelashes. Let the faerie creeper think I was a dull-witted human. I was only going to finish out this one dance and then tell him to get lost. I sure as hell wasn't going to tell him my real name; I wasn't stupid. There's power in a name, especially for stalkers and magic wielding fae.

"Well, you can call me Robby," he said.

Puck, or Robby, or whatever bent down and I watched his lips descend toward me like two bloated worms. Oh hell no. This had gone way too far. I was not kissing this guy.

I sucked in rapid puffs of air and belched. Puck frowned and I pulled away, one hand flying to my mouth. I placed my other hand on my stomach and blushed.

"I am so sorry!" I said. "Wow, how embarrassing. I should never drink beer. Do you think we could go sit down? I don't feel so good."

Actually, now that the faerie creeper wasn't trying to kiss me, I felt just fine. The belching was a childhood trick. I'd been able to suck in air and belch the ABCs better than all the neighborhood boys. Who knew it would come in handy getting rid of a faerie?

"Sure," he said, smile returning to his face. "Let me buy you a proper drink. No beer."

He guided me back to the bar, his hand on my ass. I didn't want a drink, but if it got us off the dance floor, I could turn him down at the bar.

"Back so soon?" Ivy asked.

"Your friend wasn't feeling well," Puck said, reaching over the bar and grabbing a bottle of vodka. I could hear the sound of liquid pouring into a glass and he turned around holding a drink out toward me. "Here, this will help settle your stomach."

I'd never heard of vodka settling a person's stomach and was trying to come up with a way to politely turn down the drink when Ivy solved the problem for me.

"Cheers!" she exclaimed.

She crashed her glass into the one in Puck's hand, knocking the contents to the floor.

"Oopsie," she said, listing precariously on her barstool.

"How much have you had to drink?" I asked, moving toward my friend. Ivy hardly ever drank, she was too much of a control freak to get sloppy drunk, but she certainly looked wasted now.

"Just a few drinks," she said, flashing a silly grin. "I love you guys!"

Ivy opened her arms wide—considering her touch phobia, if she tried to give us a hug, she was drunk for sure—and fell off her stool onto the vodka soaked floor. Puck glared back and forth between me, Ivy, and the broken glass, his hands clenching fitfully.

"Um, sorry, Robby," I said. "Looks like I better get my friend home. Thanks for the dance."

"Wait, we never had that drink," he said, his frown again eclipsed by that dimpled smile mask.

"Rain check," I said, pasting on a false smile of my own.

He shrugged.

"Sure," he said. "I have business to attend to. Some other time."

He flapped his hand in dismissal and walked away, heading toward one of the vampires who'd approached us on the dance floor.

"You okay?" I asked, turning back to my vodka soaked friend. I shook my head. She was a mess. "We better get you out of here. Good thing you wore pants, or Kaye would be picking glass out of your butt tonight."

Ivy stayed on the floor, watching Puck through the curtain of her hair.

"I'm not drunk," she whispered.

Puck handed something to the vamp and moved on, making his way to a door at the end of the bar. When he was out of sight, Ivy stood and brushed off her jeans. She grimaced at the wet denim, grabbed two small, wooden stakes from her belt, pulled her hair up into a tight twist, and used the stakes to secure her hair at the back of her head. Crap, I knew that habit. It was what she did just before weapons training. I had a feeling we'd just stumbled on a case. Ivy was gearing up for a fight.

"What's going on?" I asked.

"I watched Puck dose your drink," she said.

Now Ivy's drunken act made sense. If she hadn't knocked the glass to the floor, I might have taken a sip.

"Why would a faerie want to ruffie me?" I asked. "Can't they just use their magic powers, or something?"

"Yes, but I imagine using that kind of magic wouldn't go unnoticed and is against the club rules," she said. "He'd need you to willingly go with him somewhere away from the watchful eyes of club security."

I shuddered, remembering the key in Puck's hands as he went through the back door.

"Somewhere like a locked storeroom?" I asked, not liking where this was going.

"Who knows how long he's been going around drugging girls," Ivy said through clenched teeth. "If there's a chance he's done this before, there could be girls like us who he's drugged in that back room. I'm not leaving without checking it out."

"What about club security?" I asked. "Can't we just tip them off?"

"We have no proof," Ivy said. Ivy poked at the shards of glass with her boot, scowling at the floor. The alcohol had already evaporated, probably taking any evidence of drugs with it. "And faeries take things like honor and reputation very seriously. If we falsely accuse Puck without solid evidence, we could be up on charges of slander. I don't even think our demon attorney friend could help us then."

I looked around for Forneus, but the demon was nowhere in sight. Leave it to the jerk to take off right when he might have been useful.

"Okay, so what do you suggest?" I asked, slinging my crossbow over my shoulder.

"I want to check out that back room," she said. "But if you don't want to come with me, I can ask Torn to walk you out. He's around here somewhere. I saw him flirting with a nymph not long ago."

"No way," I said, hands on my hips. "I'm going with you. It could have been me in that back room. I want to help. But, you know, Torn's your ally. Couldn't you ask him to come with us? He's useful in a fight and we have no idea what to expect behind that door."

Ivy ran a gloved hand over her face and sighed.

"You're right," she said. "He'll probably refuse, but it wouldn't hurt to ask. Wait here. I'll be right back."

I nodded and Ivy took off, using her faerie quickness and agility to flit through the thickening crowd. I soon lost sight of my friend and turned my attention to the door that Puck had gone through earlier. I watched a vampire leave the bar and swagger toward the door. He was wearing snakeskin boots, dark jeans, and a black fedora. Holding my breath, I moved further down the bar, hoping for a glimpse into the room beyond.

A beautiful, blue-skinned faerie upended a shot glass of something dark amber onto an armful of linens and raced over to the door. The vampire scowled, but held the door for the faerie who rushed inside. The vamp followed close at her heels, the door snapping shut behind him.

I was trying to figure out how to get inside that locked door when my jaw dropped open. Forneus strode forward and tried to push a key into the lock. How the heck did the demon get a key? Was he part of this whole date rape drug thing? If he was, I had a holy water dipped crossbow bolt with his name on it.

He seemed to be having trouble with the key. I moved even closer as he focused on the lock. A tiny flame rose from Forneus' index finger and he touched it to the lock. This time when he tried the key, the door opened. The door was at the wrong angle for me to see inside, but I figured that meant whoever was behind the door couldn't see me either.

I leapt at the door as it swung shut, grasping the doorknob just before the lock could click. I let out a shaky breath, wondering what I should do next. Ivy would be here soon, hopefully with Torn in tow, and I should probably wait. But the thought of Forneus taking advantage of some poor, drugged girl clouded my vision.

I slipped through the doorway, pulled a stake from my bag, and used it to keep the door wedged open. Ivy would recognize the weapon, and would know I was inside. At least, that was the plan. She could just think it was a chunk of wood.

I shook my head and pressed my lips together. No, Ivy was good at finding people—it's what she does. She'd be able to read the clues and figure out where I'd gone. I turned away from the sliver of light coming from the bar and blinked into the darkness. I slung my crossbow from my shoulder, pushed off the safety, and stepped quietly into the room.

I stubbed my toe on a metal rack and banged my shin on a wooden crate, but I stifled the urge to cry out. I was used to bumps and bruises, but I hoped like hell that none of the cuts had drawn blood. I knew of at least one vamp who had come through this way, and there could be more below. Heck, there could be a whole nest of bloodsuckers down there.

I wiped clammy hands down the front of my dress and picked my way through the darkness. I focused on getting to the stairway that I'd glimpsed when I'd first opened the door. Too bad reaching the stairs wasn't much improvement. In fact, it was pretty freaking terrifying.

I stared down from the landing, but it was black as bat wings down there and sounds echoed up the stairway like it was a pipeline to Hell. Moans, cries, whimpers, and manic laughter mingled into a nightmarish choir that set my heart pounding in my chest.

What the heck was I doing here? I'd gotten myself into a lot of messes, but this one might just take the cake, the icing, and the whole damn serving plate.

I hesitated, one foot hovering over empty air as I considered retreating back to the storeroom. Waiting for Ivy would be the smart thing, which was probably why Fate propelled me down the stairs at the sound of Forneus speaking to someone below.

My nickname? Yeah, it was more than just a catchy moniker. Me and Lady Luck have never been close. In fact, we were fast becoming frenemies, which was the likely cause of my attraction to the demon speaking below.

I recognized Forneus' voice, but I was too far away to make out the words. *If I could just get a little closer...* I teetered on one platform sandal and sighed. If I was going to go tiptoeing through the dark, I probably shouldn't be wearing these shoes.

I slipped out of my platform sandals and grimaced as something crunched beneath my feet. But stepping on spiders and cockroaches was the least of my worries. I needed to find out what Forneus and Puck were up to, preferably without twisting my ankle or taking a tumble into the basement below.

With my bad luck, I'd break my ankle *and* my neck.

I grabbed the old, splintered railing and began my slow descent down the stairs. Goosebumps dotted my skin and I shivered as a heavy quiet seemed to swallow the basement. The cries and whimpers had stopped. That should have been an improvement, but the dead air was even worse than the sounds of torment.

Forneus' voice broke the silence, followed by Puck's laughter. I shuddered at the ghoulish images that conjured up. Were they hurting innocent people down here? I didn't want to believe it, but Ivy had seen Puck try to dose my drink and though Forneus was smoking hot, he was still a freaking demon. And demons were evil, right?

I paused as I ran out of stairs. I'd reached the lower basement level, and though a faint light shone from the room beyond, I couldn't make out much of the chamber I was in. I inched forward, keeping my hand on the wall. I didn't have supernatural eyesight like Forneus or Puck. If I wanted to see what was really going on, I'd have to get closer to the light.

I started forward, but jumped as a shadow broke away from the wall. Entering the room beyond, the dark shape became a tall, blue-skinned faerie woman. Huh, that was odd. It was the same chick who'd been tending bar.

I'd wondered where the faerie and vampire had disappeared to, but I'd assumed the two had come down here together. In fact, I had some pretty icky ideas when I'd seen them sneak off into the basement. Thankfully, whatever the faerie was up to, it didn't include getting naked with a vampire. There are some things I just didn't need to see. If what Ivy had said about vamps being dried out corpses was true, vampire sex was definitely on my list of things to avoid at all cost. A girl can only handle so many nightmares.

I was startled from my musing as the faerie woman leapt into the room beyond. I hurried to the corner she'd vacated, hoping for a better look. The bartender charged toward Puck, yelling and laughing maniacally, arm raised above her head. There was something shiny clutched in her fist, some kind of weapon, but she never had a chance to stab anyone.

Faster than my human eyes could follow, a vampire came rushing out of an adjacent room. A door whipped open and suddenly he was there, standing between the woman and Puck—the woman's bleeding arm held in the vampire's fist.

I leaned against the wall, knees weak. I took a deep breath, trying to slow my racing heart, and blinked away dark spots in my vision. There was at least one killer in the next room. I could not pass out.

I placed shaky hands on my knees and gulped in air. When I finally trusted myself to stand, I lifted my crossbow to my shoulder and peered around the corner. A lot had happened while I'd struggled to stay conscious.

Puck lay bleeding on the floor, something metallic jutting from his chest, and the vampire was holding the faerie woman upright while he feasted on her jugular. It was the same vamp I'd seen earlier, though he'd lost his hat and the look of calm, southern charm.

I didn't know what kind of mess the faerie had got herself into, but no one deserved to become some vamp's chew toy. Heck, he'd torn off her arm and was sucking on the faerie bartender's neck like a toddler with a god damned sippy cup.

I tuned out the slurping sounds and ran into the room. Forneus' eyes widened, and I couldn't help but grin. For once, I'd surprised the unflappable demon. But I couldn't revel in the moment; it didn't seem wise to keep the sounds of feeding at my back.

I swung the crossbow around to point at the vampire.

"Move away from the girl, douchebag," I said.

The slurping stopped and the vamp tossed the woman aside like a crumpled up juice box. I glared at the vampire, careful to keep from looking him directly in the eye, and my finger twitched on the trigger mechanism of my bow. Who died and gave him the right to treat people as if they were disposable?

Oh, right. He did, and then he rose again. Well, the bastard should have stayed dead. One dead vamp, coming right up.

The vampire was rushing forward before I could finish pulling the trigger. That doesn't mean I didn't get off a shot. I hit him square in the chest. Too bad I'd loaded for demons.

A wooden bolt would have paralyzed the vampire, but the metal I shot him with didn't even slow the guy down. I was going to die and I wasn't even wearing shoes. There was something tragic about facing death in your bare feet.

Thankfully, it wasn't my day to die. One second I was about to have my heart ripped out and the next I was shoved against the wall. The vampire's claws had been so close to my chest, I was scared to look down. I took a breath and felt the front of my dress, surprised it wasn't covered in blood. My shoulder hurt like hell, but I was alive.

I stared across the room where Forneus stood over the vampire—the vampire who had just tried to kill me—the demon's walking stick thrust through the vamp's chest.

Forneus had saved my life.

I'd finally got my answer. Not all demons are evil. When it mattered, Forneus had risked his life to save my own.

As I'd often fantasized, there was the trace of a good man under that bad boy exterior. The demon was no Boy Scout, but then, what would be the fun in that?

I gazed into Forneus' worried stare and warmth spread through my body. As he came closer, my hands twitched, aching to grab hold of his powerful arms, and then run them along his chest, his back,...

"Are you alright?" he asked.

I nodded, blushing painfully, and pushed away from the wall.

"Yes, I'm fine," I said. I pointed at the faerie woman's corpse crumpled on the ground, like a fallen ragdoll, just a few feet away. "But I can't say the same for her. We need to get her to a hospital."

Forneus winced and looked away.

"I'm sorry, my dear," he said. "She's dead."

"Um, okay, and him?" I asked, pointing toward the vampire.

Forneus had creatively used his wooden walking stick to stake the vamp through the heart, but I was pretty sure that didn't mean the bloodsucker was dead. It takes a lot to kill a vamp. But I suppose if paranormals were easy to kill, then Jenna and her Hunter friends would be out of a job.

"Oh, he is still very much alive...as alive as any undead creature ever really is," he said, walking over with measured steps to stand over the vampire.

"You've been a very naughty boy," he said, glaring down at the vampire. "I'm sure the Vampire Council will be interested to learn of your arrogant disregard for the law."

The vamp's eyes flicked to what I'd come to think of as "the torture room." I'd only caught a glimpse of the room as I chased after the faerie woman, looking for potential threats. Forneus walked over to investigate, but I stayed put. One glimpse into that room was more than enough.

Forneus' shoulders tightened and he pulled the door closed.

"Yes, the Council will be very interested indeed," he said. "Too bad they won't have a chance to punish you for your crimes."

He spun on his heel, flame dancing along his fingers, and returned to loom over the vamp.

"Say hello to Lucifer for me," he said to the vamp. "I'm sure the two of you will soon be well acquainted."

He pulled the walking stick from the vamp's heart and placed a fiery hand on his chest. Within seconds the vamp was replaced by flames and, finally, ash.

Forneus looked away, brushing vamp ash from his hands and tugging on a glove he pulled from his coat pocket. I wanted him to look at me, to give me the chance to show him how I felt. He'd saved my life and given me hope that my feelings for him were more than misdirected rebellion.

"Thank you," I said.

I stepped into his arms, hands sliding across his chest. I licked my lips, tilted my head back, and looked him in the eye.

"For what?" he asked, voice uncertain.

"For killing that creature, for looking out for me, for saving my life," I said.

I reached up to touch his face, letting my fingers linger as I slowly traced his lips, jaw, and neck. He was like a puzzle I'd only just started to figure out—the separate, distinct parts of him coming together for a complete picture that overwhelmed the senses.

Forneus sucked in a breath and I hesitated, pulling back slightly. Had I somehow offended him? Had I gone too far? Did he think I was only doing this out of some sense of duty, to thank him for saving my life?

"I am always at your service," he said softly, leaning closer. "If you will have me."

I could feel a slow smile touch my lips as my breath quickened. I pulled him closer and rose on tiptoes to meet his scorching gaze.

"Yes, Forneus, I will," I said, letting my lips brush against his.

Forneus groaned as I slanted my mouth across his, heat flowing between us. His hands moved in slow circles down my back, pulling me closer. My lips parted and our kiss deepened.

It was a good thing Forneus was immortal, because I could kiss the man forever.

But all good things come to an end. I heard Ivy bust into the room, swearing, "Oh hell, no." Forneus and I broke apart to see Ivy and Torn both rush into the room and take in the grisly scene. I reluctantly stepped away from Forneus.

Ivy narrowed her eyes and focused her attention on me. "Are you okay?" she asked.

I nodded, pausing to catch my breath. That had been one amazing kiss.

"Yes, I'm fine," I said. "Thanks to Forneus. You were right about Puck. The guy was an asshat. I didn't catch all the details, but I'm pretty sure he was drugging and selling girls to sicko vamps who got off on torture." I bit my lip and stole a glance at Forneus. "I saw that girl...hanging in the other room, but I appreciate what you tried to do."

"I only wish I'd arrived sooner," he said. He reached out and took my hand. "I would have preferred to have saved the girl and to have kept you from seeing the depths of such depravity."

I gave his hand a squeeze and looked searchingly into his eyes. How could I have been so blind as to think this man was a monster?

I wanted to pull him close and forget about my friend's stares and the corpses littering the floor, but something latched onto my hair. Pain seared through my scalp and I gasped. A true monster had me in his grasp and my crossbow was out of reach.

I felt the bite of a blade against my neck, and then everything went black.

DEMONIZED

The ogre glared at me from beneath his unfortunate simian brow, waiting for my response. His considerable bulk blocked the entrance to Club Nexus and one sizable hand twitched over the gun strapped to his barrel-like chest. Subtlety was not an ogre's strong suit. Speaking of suits, this creature's taste ran toward pimp chic. The fabric was cheap and shiny, reflecting light from the single working bulb on this street.

"Forneus, Great Marquis of Hell," I said, focusing on the bouncer's beady eyes and avoiding being blinded by his hideous taste in fashion.

The ogre leaned forward, sniffed at the air with a nose the size of a Volkswagen Beetle, and grimaced. *Unpleasant oaf.* Apparently, he didn't care for the aroma of fresh brimstone. Of course, I could mask the sulfurous scent of Hell, but where would be the fun in that? The ogre examined me from head to impeccably dressed toe.

"Don't get many demon lords here," he said, furrowing his substantial brow.

"No, I daresay you wouldn't," I said. "Not with that witch working with the Hunters' Guild to maintain their so-called peace over the entire city of Harborsmouth."

The ogre spat, narrowly missing my shoes. Now it was my turn to grimace. The cretin had utterly appalling manners. Dressing an ogre in a cut-rate suit does not a gentleman make. Before the vile creature could cough up any more distressing substances, I waved toward the door and forced a smile.

"May I enter?" I asked.

A clipboard materialized from thin air, but I was unimpressed. I'd been using the same trick with clients for eons. I tapped my foot, careful to avoid the pile of phlegm that rivaled the size of most cats—perhaps it actually was a cat?— as the ogre consulted his magical guest list.

Finally, the hulking faerie stepped aside and muttered, "You may enter."

I smoothed the front of my waistcoat, tugged at my gloves, and took up my ebony walking stick. The ogre didn't check the polished wood and therefore did not discover the sword hidden within its shaft, which was for the best. Weapons were not entirely forbidden inside the club, just unauthorized bloodshed, but I preferred to keep my secrets. You never know when you'll need a little surprise up your sleeve or, as in this case, inside your perambulatory accessory.

Plus, the hidden blade was made of cold iron. Iron was the one weakness of all fae creatures, a vulnerability that would leave any faerie who touched it powerless. If the ogre tried to handle my sword, he'd get a truly unpleasant surprise.

Hell help any faerie run through with cold iron. The Fair Folk may be immortal, but they are not immune to a painful death. I grinned and walked jauntily past the ogre, into a dark passage and onto an extravagantly wrought spiral staircase where I began my descent into the abyss of otherworldly delights.

From my aerial vantage, I took in the appalling number of fae housed beneath one cavernous roof. Though I rarely grace the establishment with my presence—my last trip below must have been years ago—not much had changed since my earlier visit to the raucous nightclub. Immortals are not fond of change.

Unnatural music wove through the air like dancing phantasms, reaching its spectral fingers into dark places better left untouched. I gritted my teeth and stifled the urge to tap my boots to the discordant rhythm. I searched the room for the woman I'd followed here, an unfamiliar sense of foreboding filling my chest.

It had been centuries since a human had piqued my interest, longer still since anyone had stirred feelings of lust and longing, but there was something unquestionably magnetic about the woman my eyes now frantically sought.

Jinx had entered Club Nexus with her friend, and business partner, Ivy Granger. Granger was a dangerous enough companion, but Jinx's decision to enter the fae nightclub was nearly suicidal. Faeries and vampires both enjoy the diversion of a winsome human and Jinx was an absolute vision of beauty.

Lucifer's pointy pitchfork, what is wrong with the woman?

I gripped my walking stick in a stranglehold until my eyes fell on Jinx and her psychic detective friend seated at the bar. I hurriedly made my way down the stairs, slowing only as I crossed the dance floor. I licked my lips, shivering in anticipation.

I'd come here to ensure the woman's safety, but now that she was within reach, I was overcome with the need to feel her touch—even if I'd have to settle for a crossbow bolt through the chest. One gloved hand drifted to my side where I'd recently received the sharp end of a letter opener. Jinx was nothing if not feisty.

I sauntered to the bar, smiling when Jinx caught my hungry gaze. For a startled moment, her face was an open book and her expression mirrored my own. Desire smoldered in her eyes as she absently stroked the crossbow at her shoulder.

"Hello, sweetheart," I said, slipping an arm around her shoulders. "Buy you a drink?"

My words were cut off abruptly by a knife at my throat. Ivy had gone from ordering drinks to threatening violence. From Jinx it would have been enticing, but coming from her glowing friend, the gesture was maddeningly annoying.

There was a minor altercation with club security for engaging in violent behavior—behavior that threatened bloodshed without having first filed the appropriate paperwork (yawn)—but eventually, I extricated myself from Ivy's blade, slipping my arm from Jinx's shoulders with a look that promised a rematch later in the evening. Our business was not complete, but, for now, I was content to watch from the sidelines. The prudent course of action was to wait for Ivy to calm down and for club security to lose interest.

Not a problem. I could be very, very patient.

I sauntered away from the bar and settled in to wait. Unfortunately, my patience was rewarded by the appearance of Puck. I cursed under my breath, hands twitching along the catch that would release my sword from its wooden sheath. Whatever that trickster wanted with Jinx, it couldn't be good. I pushed my way through the crowd, hoping to catch their conversation.

I stopped mid-stride, head snapping back as if slapped by an invisible hand, as Jinx led the angelic looking faerie onto the dance floor. If the reverse had been true, I'd have sliced Puck's hand off—and to Hell with the consequences—but Jinx was acting as the aggressor. I hoped she lived long enough to regret the dubious decision.

I briefly closed my eyes and had to look away when Puck's hands settled on Jinx's full hips. I never thought I'd envy the trickster, but at the moment I'd pay handsomely to trade places with the predatory scoundrel. I paced restlessly, gathering the courage to continue my observations.

When I looked back, Jinx and Puck were leaving the dance floor, heading back toward the bar. I followed at a careful distance, not wanting to alert Puck to my presence.

I tried not to focus on Puck's hand resting possessively around Jinx's waist. I didn't wish to see any additional displays of affection from my rival, but I had come to ensure Jinx's safety and that was a duty I would carry out, no matter how vexing the task.

At the bar, Puck proceeded to fix a drink for Jinx and I expelled a pained breath as I watched the white powder dissolve in her glass. This was too much to bear. The trickster was trying to drug the woman I'd come here to protect. I launched myself forward, ready to knock the glass from Jinx's hand, but I never had the chance.

Before I could reach the bar, Ivy toasted Jinx and Puck, knocking the drugged beverage to the floor. Moments later, Ivy swayed drunkenly on her stool and tumbled to join the puddle of alcohol and shattered glass.

What the Hellfire was going on?

I wasn't sure what Ivy was up to—had she also caught a glimpse of Puck's attempt to drug Jinx?—but I knew the detective well enough to guess that her drunkenness was a ruse. Jinx's friend was more uptight than a Puritan in a bordello. She'd never willingly drink enough alcohol to lose control, certainly not here in a club filled with immortals carrying millennia of potential nightmare visions.

I tugged at my gloves, a slow smile replacing my earlier scowl. I may not know what game Ivy was playing at, but I did enjoy the temporary result. Puck was frowning, his hands opening and closing at his sides as if he'd like to wring the wisp princess' neck. Well, we've all felt that way at some time or other, but at the moment I was quite pleased with the woman's performance. Anything that angered the trickster was splendid in my book.

As I watched, Puck left Jinx's side, stalking away from the bar and toward a vampire who stood waiting at the edge of the dance floor. I followed at a discreet distance, humming and twirling my walking stick to the music, the very image of blithe ignorance. He passed a key and a small bag containing a white, powdery substance to the vampire and kept moving.

Puck continued on toward a door at the back of the bar. He looked furtively to his left and right, slid a key of his own from his pants' pocket, and unlocked the door. With one last glance around the room, the faerie slipped inside.

My curiosity was piqued. The trickster's behavior was interesting, indeed. Puck may have pulled the wool over Jinx's eyes, but I knew what he was capable of. If he was sneaking off into the back rooms instead of fawning over a pretty woman, no matter how annoying her friend, he must be up to something particularly despicable. Perhaps if I could catch him in an act of heinous trickery, I could convince Jinx to keep her distance from the cretin.

At the edge of the dance floor, my walking stick caught on an imaginary bump in the floor and I stumbled forward into the arms of the vampire I'd witnessed make the recent transaction with Puck. I brushed off the vampire as if ridding him of demon germs, patting him down and retrieving his key in the process, and muttered an effusive apology.

The man raised a hand as if to push me away, but froze when I allowed a flicker of flame into my eyes. There was one thing that all vampires fear and that is fire, immolation being a very real threat to the perpetually dehydrated undead. Satisfactorily humbled, the vampire accepted my apology and I continued on my way, nonchalantly following Puck's trail across the room.

I approached the door he'd entered, aware that Jinx remained with Ivy at the opposite end of the bar. With her best friend watching her back and Sir Torn, one of Ivy's new allies, nearby, I felt confident leaving Jinx in the club while I pursued Goodfellow.

Distracted by thoughts of Jinx, I nearly didn't notice that I was not the only one in pursuit of Puck. I pulled up short just in time, slipping between a pair of lounging succubi seconds before a vampire in cowboy boots strode to the door with his own key. As the vampire unlocked the door, a tall, beautiful faerie who'd been tending bar rushed to his side. Her arms were laden with soiled towels and she kept her eyes downcast, but I could tell she was highborn fae.

I wondered how Puck had managed to ensnare the royal faerie into the lowly position of bartender. Knowing Puck, it involved foul trickery. Even knowing the trickster's abilities, it was still surprising that he'd maneuvered himself into the position of running the club's bar. It was, judging from the transactions I'd witnessed so far, a profitable deal for Puck. If he didn't have designs on Jinx, I might even have admired the faerie's enterprising tenacity.

I waited patiently for the vampire and Unseelie faerie to disappear into the back rooms before extricating myself from the succubi.

"Ladies," I said with a nod.

The succubi, one raven-haired, the other blonde, pouted and stretched catlike, showing off their various assets, but I wasn't interested. Succubi are a dime a dozen in Hell, but a stubborn, beautiful, kind-hearted, yet somewhat violent human woman like Jinx? She was a rare gem indeed.

Leaving two sets of pouty lips behind, I stalked toward the end of the bar. Reaching the door to the back rooms, I slipped the burgled key from my pocket and attempted to fit it into the lock. Had I been mistaken about the key? I raised my brow at the difficult lock and leaned closer to see what could be the trouble. At closer inspection, I could see that the doorknob was frosted over and the lock was filled with ice.

Damn and blast, that Unseelie bartender must have used her ice magic to seal the door. I gritted my teeth at the delay and tugged the glove from my right hand. Using a miniscule amount of magic, a small flame formed from my index finger. I'd used the technique previously as a parlor trick, but the flame was just as effective at melting the ice within the lock as it had been lighting cigars. I tucked the glove into the pocket of my waistcoat and let myself inside.

I moved quickly through the storeroom located immediately behind the locked door and moved stealthily down a flight of stairs to a series of chambers below. Crates and racks of wine were soon replaced by beverages of a very different vintage.

The lower level reeked of death and I reached out with my magic, scouring the cellars for any sign of Puck. The trickster wasn't hard to find. Indeed, my search was more fruitful than I'd hoped. I'd found the leverage I needed to keep Jinx from the faerie. I should have been delighted, but instead, I found myself flushing hot with unspent anger.

I'd witnessed many horrors inflicted within the various levels of Hell. In fact, there was a time that I'd participated wholeheartedly. But my passion for inflicting pain and fear had burned out many centuries ago. Now, as I sensed the suffering perpetrated in the adjoining rooms, I had the urge to be sick. I brought a handkerchief to my face, recoiling at the stench of blood, excrement, and offal.

With the details plucked from my magical surveillance, and my observations from the adjoining club, Puck's newest business enterprise became immediately clear. He'd used his position running the nightclub to gain access to the storage rooms and cellars and had converted this space into a vile den of iniquity. He'd created a bordello for vampires and other depraved creatures whose tastes ran toward tormenting their prey before they feasted.

I was somewhat surprised to find that I was appalled by the very idea. Perhaps it was the knowledge that Jinx was not so very different from the humans who lay drugged, tortured, bleeding, or dead in the rooms beyond.

In fact, Puck had tried to drug Jinx this very night.

That mistake would lead to the trickster's downfall; Puck was going to pay dearly. I gripped my walking stick in a white-knuckled fist, my ungloved hand leaving scorch marks on the polished wood.

I closed my eyes and breathed deeply, inhaling the scent of burnt wood and blood, and turned my attention to the energy of the ley lines that converged all around me. Club Nexus was located at a magical nexus point where powerful ley lines intersected, a fact I now found fortuitous.

I reached out and plucked at the humming threads close-at-hand and smiled. These would do nicely. I latched onto two ley lines with my will and gasped as the energy jolted into my body. The experience was akin to biting down on a live wire while climaxing; it was not something a corporeal body, even that of a demon, was meant to withstand for any length of time. I drew in a considerable dose of power and, with a panting sigh, let go of the line.

I opened my eyes, unsurprised to see flickers of crimson flame dance along my fingers and up and down my sword cane. I'd drawn heavily on the ley lines, becoming a conduit of immense power. Now that power needed a place to go.

My hand tightened on the cane and I welcomed the heat rising within me. Puck had chosen the wrong mortal woman to snare in his tangled web. I lifted my chin high, thrust out my chest, and strode into the room beyond.

The room was dimly lit, but I could see that the vampire had continued on into an adjoining room where, judging by the screams and whimpering, he was enjoying himself immensely. I shifted my focus to the one man who remained in the room. The vampire, and those like him, would be dealt with, but first, I would devote myself to protecting Jinx by learning the complete nature of Puck's filthy game. I grinned, and a lick of fire and the hum of barely contained energy danced along my lips.

The source of my fury was standing dead ahead.

"Ah, Puck," I said, raising an eyebrow as I made a show of taking in my surroundings. "I thought you might be up to your old tricks. Catering to the bloodsuckers now, I see."

"Everyone has needs," Puck said with a shrug. The faerie smiled wide, but no sign of levity reached his calculating eyes. "And the undead have deep pockets. You can't blame a guy for trying to make a living."

I lifted a handkerchief to my nose and grimaced, maintaining my grip on the sword cane with my right hand. A weak, rattling, whimper rose from a nearby room and I hurried on. Vampires could move quickly and it sounded as if the Southern vamp was not a man of restraint.

If I didn't finish my business with Puck swiftly, the human source of those cries would be beyond my ability to render assistance. My mind conjured the image of a vampire sinking his fangs into pale skin decorated by a familiar rose tattoo, the phantom likeness juxtaposed with the soundtrack of pained whimpers, and heat raced through my veins.

"But I do blame you, indubitably," I said. "You have placed someone I care for in harm's way and I intend to seek suitable retribution."

"Come now, Forneus," Puck said, spreading his hands wide. "I'm sure we can come to a friendly arrangement."

I shook my head.

"I do believe we are beyond negotiating," I said, tossing the handkerchief over my shoulder. I shifted my cane into my left hand and lifted my right, allowing flame to dance along my fingers. "You see, Puck, there is an aggravating factor, a detail which makes your action particularly injurious to me, personally. But perhaps you could sway my verdict with a plea bargain."

I might be satisfied if the trickster provided enough information, and begged sufficiently.

"Playing at judge, jury, and executioner?" he asked. "That's not like you, Forneus. Heck, I didn't think you had the balls. Good for you."

As Puck said the last, his eyes held my own, but his hand slid toward his pocket. Whether he was going for a weapon, or attempting to call for backup, our discussion was evidently over. I started to flick my wrist, intending to send an onslaught of flame at the trickster's wandering hand, but halted the motion as something flew past my shoulder.

I'd been so focused on those I pursued ahead of me that I hadn't bothered to turn my attention to what might approach from behind.

I spun on my heel in time to see an enraged, blue-skinned faerie hurl herself toward Puck. The trickster's head snapped up, eyes widening, as a jeweled dagger descended toward his chest. This faerie woman, the bartender from the club if I wasn't mistaken, obviously intended to kill the trickster. I can't say I could blame her. The boyish looking man had an appalling habit of screwing over everyone he encountered.

In a rainbow arc of shining jewels, the weapon plunged downward, but the motion was arrested when a dusty, fanged blur interceded. With a snarl, the southern vampire grabbed the bartender's arm and ripped it off at the shoulder. Blood sprayed from the ragged wound, making an unseemly mess, but the vampire's intervention was effective. Puck was unharmed, though I couldn't say the same for his clothing.

Unfortunately, the sight of so much blood pushed the vampire into a feeding frenzy. The vampire's fangs elongated further and, with a growl, he latched himself onto the woman's neck.

"Stop this at once!" I demanded. "Puck, this has gone too far. She's a faerie, one of your own kind."

Puck rocked his head back and laughed.

"One of my kind?" he asked. He stepped closer to where the vampire feasted on the injured faerie woman. "She's an Unseelie, one of Mab's brood. Their kind aren't worth saving."

"This is against club rules and Vampire Law," I said, attempting one last time to appeal to reason. "Stop this and give up this wretched game of yours."

"No, Forneus, I'm having too much fun to close down my little Bite Club," Puck said. "Our activities are profitable, and I provide a much-needed service to the vampire community. Isn't that right, Cyrus?"

The vampire paused at his name, but soon continued to suckle at the faerie's neck, holding her upright in a parody of a lover's embrace. The winter faerie's blue skin made it difficult to tell if she was still alive, but the loss of blood from the missing limb, and the vampire latched onto her neck like an engorged tick, would kill her soon if it hadn't already. This had to be stopped.

Once again I began to flick my wrist and once again the faerie woman interceded. Silver flashed in the dim light and a blue hand thrust upward, striking Puck in the chest. The makeshift weapon, an ice pick if I wasn't mistaken, was driven deeply as the faerie smiled.

Apparently, the woman was alive, after all.

"I did as you asked, my queen," she rasped.

I didn't have time to ponder those words, though I planned to investigate the matter further as soon as the opportunity arose. Whether Mab walked the mortal world was a detail worth knowing.

Puck fell to the floor, the ice pick standing from his chest like a flagpole. At Puck's apparent demise, the vampire shrieked and tore at the faerie woman's clothing. I shook my head and grimaced as skin and fabric began to shred into streamers of bloody confetti.

"You really shouldn't play with your food," I said. "It's ghastly manners."

Flame danced along my fingers and I raised my arm toward the vampire. Fire was one of the few ways to deal with the undead, and it was something I had in abundance.

The sound of heavy breathing registered just as I smelled Jinx's unique scent. She ran into the room, a loaded crossbow held at the ready. She aimed the bow at me, but wavered as she took in the grisly scene.

What the devil?

"Move away from the girl, douchebag," she said, shifting her aim to the vampire.

Cyrus let the drained faerie's corpse drop to the floor, tossing it aside like a sack of rubbish. Jinx blanched at the sight of the vampire's blood-smeared face, but kept her eyes focused steadily on his gore-covered chin—clever girl. She may be impetuous, but at least she had the wherewithal to avoid the vampire's mesmeric gaze.

I might have been pleased by her sudden appearance if she hadn't placed herself unmistakably in harm's way. Aiming one's weapon, especially one filled with pointy objects, at a blood-crazed predator was not generally looked upon as a wise course of action. Not unless you struck without hesitation.

"Might I suggest stepping aside?" I asked, hoping she'd take my advice. Jinx stood squarely in my way. I couldn't unleash the flames in my grasp without risking her safety.

The vampire, Cyrus, held himself completely still, head tilted as he sized up the situation. Unless Jinx had brought an army of Hunters as backup, we were running out of time. Soon the vampire would discern that, except for a basement full of corpses, we were quite alone. I could not use fire as a weapon without striking Jinx and she stood too close to the vampire to get off more than one shot with her crossbow.

That made Jinx easy prey.

In a blur of movement, the vampire snarled and rushed toward Jinx, razor-tipped fingers extended like claws. I spun to the right and propelled myself forward, hoping to close the distance and intercede before the vampire reached his target.

I heard the twang of a bowstring a mere second before a stain blossomed on the vampire's chest. It was an admirable shot, the crossbow bolt going straight through the heart, but the bolt must not have been made of wood. The vampire continued moving forward.

Heart pounding, I lunged, pushed Jinx aside, and rammed the shaft of my walking stick through the vampire's chest. In this case, the walking stick was more effective than the sword it encased. A wooden stake, or rather my wooden walking stick, causes paralysis when driven through the heart of a vampire. My sword would have done nothing more than anger the creature.

Now the vampire was pinned to the floor like a ghoulish specimen. I had no idea what to do with the man, but such decisions could wait. Cyrus wouldn't be going anywhere soon. The vampire would keep.

Instead, I rushed to where Jinx leaned against a nearby wall. I'd pushed her away from the vampire as gently as I could, but I was a demon filled with the hum of immense ley line power. Jinx was strong, but she was human. I hoped she hadn't sustained any serious injuries while I'd dispatched her opponent.

"Are you alright?" I asked.

Jinx shook her head, smiled ruefully, and pushed herself away from the wall.

"Yes, I'm fine," she said. She gestured toward the faerie woman's corpse at our feet. "But I can't say the same for her. We need to get her to a hospital."

The faerie woman was beyond the services of any medical institution, I'd noted the moment when her heart had ceased to beat, but I made a show of checking her pulse. No sense reminding Jinx of how very different we were from each other. I could share my ability to feel the transcendence of a soul from the flesh in a later conversation—if there was a later. I just hoped that she had come to the realization that I'd had no part in Puck's blood sport.

"I'm sorry, my dear," I said. "She's dead."

Jinx flashed a pained look, but covered it quickly. She nodded and continued to take in the grisly scene.

"And him?" she asked, pointing toward the vampire, my walking stick holding him immobile.

"Oh, he is still very much alive…as alive as any undead creature ever really is," I said, moving toward the vampire.

I smelt the layers of death on him. This one had taken hundreds of lives, and reveled in it.

"You've been a very naughty boy," I said, staring down at the vampire. "I'm sure the Vampire Council will be interested to learn of your arrogant disregard for the law."

His eyes flicked toward an open door and I turned to see a young girl hanging from the wall, her wrists shackled to the stone. Ribbons of flesh dangled from her naked body where it hung beside a table of sharp instruments. The girl had been tortured and then drained of blood.

I grimaced, walked stiffly to the room, and closed the door. The girl was beyond saving, her life already expired, but perhaps I could shield Jinx from witnessing such horror.

"Yes, the council will be very interested indeed," I said. "Too bad they won't have a chance to punish you for your crimes."

Flame danced along my fingers as I walked back to where the vampire lay impaled by my walking stick.

"Say hello to Lucifer for me," I said, letting my lips curl in a grin. "I'm sure the two of you will soon be well acquainted."

I pulled my walking stick from his heart and placed a fiery hand on his chest. The vampire immediately caught fire, burning to ash within seconds.

I stood and brushed dust and ash from my hand, slipped the glove from my waistcoat pocket, and tugged it on. I took my time, afraid to see the judgment waiting in Jinx's eyes. I'd made my decision to terminate the vampire when I smelt his ecstasy in the room where the tortured girl still hung. A rogue vampire would never change, only becoming more twisted over time, but Jinx may not know that. All she'd seen was a demon burn a man alive.

How could she possibly accept me after witnessing such a gruesome sight?

I sighed, raking a hand through my hair. Might as well get on with it, I noted grimly. I pasted a smile on my face and spun around, hoping to make light of the situation, but Jinx wasn't scowling in disgust or wringing her hands. I relaxed as a slow smile spread across her face.

"Thank you," she said.

Jinx stepped into my arms and tilted her head back to look me in the eye.

"For what?" I asked, dumbfounded. For once, I, the great Forneus, Great Marquis of Hell, was at a loss for words.

"For killing that creature, for looking out for me, for saving my life," she said.

Jinx reached up to touch my face, her fingers tracing my lips, my jaw, and down my neck. Her lingering touch was excruciatingly tender. I sucked in a breath, afraid to move for fear of breaking the spell that granted me my innermost desire.

She raised an eyebrow and I struggled to think of an appropriate response. But my body didn't want to reply with words.

"I am always at your service," I said softly, leaning closer. "If you will have me."

Jinx lifted herself onto tiptoe, closing the distance between us.

"Yes, Forneus, I will," she said, lips brushing mine.

I groaned as she tilted her head, slanting her mouth across my own. I ran my hands over her bare shoulders, fingers tracing the tattooed skin. They continued their descent down her back, pulling her closer. Her lips parted, and our kiss deepened. *Oh, great Lucifer, yes!* I could spend eternity kissing Jinx.

Too bad her friends chose that moment to interrupt.

Ivy and Torn rushed into the room, yelling for Jinx and brandishing weapons. As Jinx and I parted—eyes glassy and skin flushed, I daresay—her friends took in the crumpled bodies of Puck, the Unseelie bartender, and the vampire-shaped pile of ash.

Ivy's eyes darted around the room, finally landing on her friend.

"Are you okay?" Ivy asked.

Jinx blinked and slowly nodded.

"Yes, I'm fine," she said. "Thanks to Forneus. You were right about Puck. The guy was an asshat. I didn't catch all the details, but I'm pretty sure he was drugging and selling girls to sicko vamps who got off on torture." She bit her lip and flicked her eyes my way. "I saw that girl...hanging in the other room, but I appreciate what you tried to do."

Ah, so I hadn't been quick enough in my attempt to hide the terrors of the tortured girl behind the closed door. Jinx was tough—it was one of the many qualities I adored—but I'd hoped to spare her that particular nightmare.

"I only wish I'd arrived sooner," I said, reaching for her hand. "I would have preferred to have saved the girl and to have kept you from seeing the depths of such depravity."

She gave my hand a light squeeze, face upturned. I wanted to pull her to me, but I never had the chance.

Puck, like a cat with nine lives, sprung to his feet and pounced on Jinx from behind. We'd made a terrible mistake; the trickster was not dead, only wounded. I should have reached out with my demon magic and searched his body for a soul, but I hadn't been paying attention—and now the trickster was armed.

He'd pulled the ice pick from his chest and had retrieved the jeweled dagger from the Unseelie faerie's lifeless hand. The amputated arm carrying the blade had been tossed aside by the vampire and I hadn't spared it a second thought.

If harm came to Jinx, it would be my fault for not being more thorough. Lucifer knows, I should have checked Puck's body for signs of life, but I'd been too distracted by my own desire. I'd given the trickster the perfect opportunity for revenge.

Ivy and Torn had apparently come to the same conclusion.

With painful clarity, I took in the details of the situation. Ivy's face paled and her skin began to glow. Her hair lifted to dance around her head with unspent magical energy, but the wisp princess hadn't yet learned how to direct the powers she'd inherited from her faerie father.

She was, however, skilled at slicing, dicing, and bashing things over the head.

Throwing knives slid from wrist sheaths to hit her palms, but at that angle, she'd be more likely to hit Jinx than Puck. She started to strafe to the side, but she'd never be fast enough, wisp powers or no.

Torn twisted in a flanking maneuver—a fierce shadow with speed to rival a cheetah—but he too had been far across the room. The cat sidhe's attack would never land in time.

There was only one person who could possibly save Jinx, and that person was me.

Jinx's eyes went wide as Puck grabbed at her hair and yanked her head back, baring her throat. The jeweled hilt of a dagger flashed in the wisp light and I knew with certainty that Puck intended to slit her throat. My mouth went dry, but I pushed away physiological distractions. Fear had no claim on me.

I was a demon.

Fire burned within my veins, building to a fever pitch, but I held it firmly with my will. I could not risk harming Jinx with jets of flame. No, I would have to be precise, methodical in the execution of my attack.

In a microsecond, I determined the most salient course of action. As Puck's blade came arcing toward Jinx's neck, my fingers still entwined with hers, I yanked her forward out of Puck's grasp. I winced at the sound of hair tearing from flesh and hoped that Jinx would forgive me later—if there was a later.

Never in all the centuries of my existence have I worried so for what the future may bring. Funny how one person could turn everything on its head.

Puck was still holding a chunk of Jinx's hair and swung his blade downward as I flung Jinx toward Torn with a flick of my wrist. The two went down with a sickening thud. When this was all over, Jinx would likely have bruises and a possible concussion to add to the bloody patch on her scalp, but my priority was saving her life. I had to hope that her friends would have the wherewithal to administer first aid. I couldn't yet risk a glance to check on her health.

I had a faerie to kill.

With Jinx out of harm's reach, I let down the rigid mental barriers I kept between myself and Hell. This time ley line power was not enough. I had to ensure that Puck would not live through this night. I would not make the mistake of underestimating the trickster again. As the mental fortifications crumbled, the screams of the damned flooded my mind. I pushed aside the echoes of torment and reached for the power that was my birthright.

Tapping into such power was not without consequence. Horns erupted from my head, ripping painfully through my scalp, and leathery wings tore through my back and clothing, ruining a perfectly good waistcoat. My cloven hooves sent up sparks where they met the basement's stone floor and I looked down at Puck with glowing eyes.

This all happened in less than a second, but the smirk had fallen from Puck's face and fear was growing behind his widening eyes. I didn't dare glance at the others in the room. I hoped that Jinx would not judge me based on my unfortunate physical transformation. This was not at all what I'd had in mind when I'd pictured our first date.

And hopefully, her friends wouldn't take it upon themselves to do a little demon hunting. The psychic detective and I had an arrangement that benefited us both, but she'd never been confronted with this form. Ivy had been raised as a human, and had human blood in her veins, and humans have an instinctual dislike for Hellspawn.

I was filled with an immeasurable amount of raw power, but this form was vulnerable on the mortal plane. If Ivy stabbed me in the back now, I would die a true death.

At least I'd had that kiss. A demon could die happy with the memory of that kiss fresh on his lips.

Speaking of dying, Puck was still alive. I'd reached out absently and held him in my grasp. Now I held his gaze and shook my head.

"I warned you before, trickster," I said. "I told you not to mess with those whom I care about. You were a fool not to heed my warning."

The souls of the damned filled my head and I pushed their anguished cries down through my veins and out through my hands—and into Puck. The faerie screamed, his face contorted, mouth open wide as the damned devoured him from within. Flames dotted his skin, charred holes forming blackened craters. In a matter of seconds, the hungry souls had added one more to their number. The physical body of Puck crumbled to ash and the souls of the damned disappeared into the stone floor, returning to Hell.

I stumbled and gripped my head, closing my eyes against the spinning room. My fingers met the warm, smooth surface of my horns and I sighed. It was time to resume what I'd come to think of as my proper form—the form Jinx might someday come to love.

There had been that kiss, after all.

Jinx had finally shown her feelings for me, but I wasn't doing our newfound relationship any good by remaining winged, horned, and cloven-hoofed. With a deep breath, I focused my will and began to rebuild the walls around the ember of Hell that resided in every demon. After a few minutes, but what felt like an eternity, I opened my eyes.

My clothing was torn, and I'd lost a shoe, but my body had returned to normal. I was Jinx's dashing suitor once again, and it was time for our heartfelt reunion. I turned toward Ivy and Torn where they hovered around Jinx's body crumpled body.

"Is she...?" I asked.

I reached out with my magic and could feel the warmth of Jinx's soul. She had not left us, not yet.

"She's alive," Torn said, brushing a stray hair from Jinx's pale face. "She's surprisingly feisty for a human."

The cat sidhe lord looked down on Jinx with such open curiosity that I had to stuff my hands inside my pockets to keep from strangling him. If Torn had any sense of self-preservation, he'd keep his distance from Jinx. Curiosity killed the cat, and all that.

"Head wound," Ivy said. "We're taking her to The Emporium. I want Kaye to have a look at her injuries."

Madame Kaye was not a fan of demons, and she was a powerful witch. Her occult shop would be heavily warded. They were taking Jinx somewhere that I couldn't follow. That left me with a hollow feeling in the pit of my stomach that I wasn't quite ready to define.

"Then let me be of assistance," I said, moving forward. "Allow me..."

Ivy held up a gloved hand and shook her head.

"I don't think that's such a good idea," she said. "Torn and I can take it from here. Plus, Kaye would sooner trap you in a circle, or blast you back to Hell, than let you cross her threshold."

"Yes, of course," I said, letting my arms hang at my sides. "You seem to have the matter well in hand."

I bit the inside of my cheek as Torn lifted Jinx into his arms. It was all I could do not to throttle the man. It should have been my chest that Jinx slumbered against, not the bone and fur laced leather vest of the unscrupulous cat sidhe.

"We do," she said, gesturing at the corpse-littered floor. "Why don't you take care of this mess and help deliver the human bodies somewhere the authorities can find them. We may not be able to explain what really happened here, but the families of the dead deserve to know that their loved ones are gone."

I'd just been relegated to the cleanup crew. How very unnerving.

"Miss Granger?" I asked. Ivy looked over her shoulder, brow raised. "Take good care of her."

"That's the idea," she said.

Ivy walked out of the basement, leaving me to the unpleasant task of informing club security about Puck's nefarious little side business.

Three days later, I entered the offices of Private Eye. I'd kept busy after that night at Club Nexus. I devoted myself to my work, closing a complex legal case and reaping enough souls to fill my annual quota, but worry over Jinx consumed me. I'd tried to be patient, to wait for her to call for me, but after the third day of pacing the streets of Harborsmouth, I'd had enough. I had to see her with my own eyes.

I had to know that she was alright.

I stepped through the door and felt my heart lighten when I saw Jinx standing beside her desk. She was busy talking with Ivy and a client, her back to me, but I could see that she was standing easily and without assistance. I observed her for a minute longer than necessary, savoring the moment when she'd turn and see me waiting for her.

Would she come rushing into my arms? I imagined the smell of her hair and the feel of her skin beneath my fingers, and smiled. I shook my head at my flights of fancy. The woman was driving me mad.

With a purposeful jingle of the door, I strode into the office. I was surprised to see that their guest was Torn, the cat sidhe lord, but I hardly paid it a thought. Ivy could keep her new ally busy. My attention was riveted on Jinx.

Jinx turned, and with a haughty toss of her head, demanded, "What are *you* doing here?"

It was not the romantic welcome I was expecting.

"Come now, darling," I said, spreading my hands wide. "Aren't we beyond this charade? I know your true feelings for me, as do your friends. They witnessed the kiss we shared. There's no sense pretending we do not care for each other."

Jinx rolled her eyes and walked to her desk. She opened the top drawer of her desk, lifted her crossbow to her shoulder, and shot me in the stomach.

"Demons," she spat, turning to Ivy. "I warned him never to call me darling."

I felt like I'd been punched in the gut, which, in fact, I had. The crossbow bolt burned, evidently having been doused in holy water, but I'd survive the wound. I was not, however, sure how I could endure Jinx's disdain.

She didn't remember our kiss.

I stood there pole-axed. She'd suffered a blow to the head and no longer remembered our kiss, that precious moment that had filled the last three days with such meaning. Jinx's loss of memory hit me with a crushing might worse than the moment Puck's blade flashed in the club's basement. An armed opponent was something I'd prepared for over the course of my long life. But how does one take up the gauntlet against something that is already lost?

Having Jinx's feelings for me ripped away was like undergoing surgery without the anesthesia. But I held onto the pain, because it was all that was left of the moment we'd shared. I wasn't willing to let her go.

I turned to Ivy, who grimaced, but met my gaze.

"Why did you keep the truth from her?" I asked. My body felt cold, but I resisted a shiver. "How could you?"

"How could I not?" she whispered. She'd spoken too softly for human ears, but now raised her voice for Jinx's benefit. "I told her all she needed to know of that night. She was attacked by Puck, but Torn and I got there in time to save her life."

Ivy had seen me transform in the basement into something out of nightmare. Fueled by Hellfire, I'd grown horns, wings, and cloven hoofs. It should not have changed anything. Jinx had known I was a demon when she'd kissed me. But Ivy apparently thought she was protecting her friend by concealing the truth.

"I will not give her up," I whispered. "And I will never forget this."

I spun on my heel, hand clutched to the crossbow bolt protruding from my stomach, and limped as gracefully as I could from the office and out onto the streets of Harborsmouth.

THRILL ON JOYSEN HILL

"**R**emind me again why I agreed to this?" Torn asked, inching away and eyeing the exits. "I'm lord of the cat sidhe, for Mab's sake!"

I shook my head and smirked.

"Because you promised to lend me your services for a few hours as a wedding gift," I said.

"Babysitting a demon toddler, a teenage troll, and a grouchy old brownie was not what I had in mind, Princess and you know it," he said.

Ceff strode into the kitchen, and I smiled, showing too many teeth. Barely restrained energies trailed along my skin and sucked the air from the already cramped apartment. Our loft had seemed spacious when it was just Jinx and me living here, but it was currently overrun with squealing kids and two overanxious soon-to-be bridegrooms. That was the problem.

When Jinx insisted on a bachelorette party, I'd surprised everyone by wholeheartedly agreeing. We were meeting Arachne at Club Nexus for a night of dancing and letting off steam. Considering that Club Nexus was a bar that attracted the denizens of Harborsmouth's supernatural underworld, chances were good I'd get a chance to try out my new wisp powers before the night was through.

At least, a girl could hope.

"So, what did you mean, Torn?" I asked, feigning innocence.

"Yes, what did you mean, Cat?" Ceff asked, narrowing his eyes.

Torn held up his hands, claws sheathed. Wise man.

"I was only giving Ivy a chance to be with a real man before she chained herself to you for all eternity, Fish Breath," he said.

Okay, not so wise. Damn Torn and his relentless flirtations. If we didn't all get a night away from each other, all hell was going to break loose and we couldn't afford any more damage to our apartment. Not with all the new mouths we had to feed.

"It's already settled," I said, raising a gloved hand. "Torn takes the kids for a few hours, Jinx and me get our bachelorette party, and Ceff and Forneus take care of the overdue loft repairs."

"I be no kid," Hob muttered from the couch, arms folded across his chest.

I winced, but turned my attention back to Torn.

"There must be something else you want for your wedding gift," he said, slit-pupil eyes pleading. "A trip to Mag Mell, untold secrets, a nice set of carving knives?"

"No, Torn," I said. "Go. Take the kids. Who knows, you might have fun."

Torn's scarred lip lifted in a lopsided grin.

"Fine, Princess, have it your way," he said, clapping his hands. "Come on kids! Let's go have some fun with Uncle Torn."

"You bring them home in one piece, Torn," I said, jabbing a gloved finger in his direction.

"Whatever, sure," he said, sauntering out the door and waving over his shoulder. "They'll be safe as houses."

I frowned, watching my kids leave the safety of our home. I'd won the argument, so why did I feel like I'd lost?

"Come on, Ivy," Jinx said, tossing me my leather jacket. "You agreed to take the night off. Torn's an immortal faerie lord with an army of cats at his beck and call. What could possibly go wrong?"

What, indeed.

*****

TORN

I hissed, muttering a curse. Every damn time I took that demon kid's hand, he zapped me, burning my skin. I was a cat sidhe lord, not a submissive underling, and these kids were overdue for a reminder of who I was. I narrowed my eyes, glaring at each of my unruly companions.

"If I find out one of you put the brat up to this, I'll flay you alive," I said, lifting my hand to show the freshly scorched flesh.

The wounds were minor. I'd suffered worse, much worse, just for the fun of it, but that wasn't the point. I had a nagging suspicion that the troll kid and the nasty little brownie were encouraging the demon child.

Hob batted his eyelashes and gave me a mocking bow.

"Never dream of it, me lord," he said with a wink.

Cheeky buggar. Faeries can't lie, but we can stretch the truth. I should know.

"Leave Sparky alone," Marvin said, lifting the demon child onto his massive shoulders. "You want trust, you earn it. Right, kiddo?"

"Baaaaaaaad man," Sparky said, pointing a sparking finger at me. "Giddy up horsey!"

I narrowed my eyes, but the troll was already galloping up the sidewalk like a buffoon. To any human passerby, Marvin appeared to be a sullen teenager in an oversized army surplus jacket and a bad haircut that hid a heavy simian brow. Sparky looked like a toddler wearing a hat with long, floppy bunny ears. That illusion might not pass scrutiny if people got concerned that the kids were being harassed by some adult predator. Shouting "bad man" seemed a fine way to get the wrong kind of attention.

"Cut that out," I hissed. "We're here to have fun, not attract attention. I might have a blithe disregard for rules, but you break the One True Law and we'll be on the Moordenaar's hit list. That, kids, is the opposite of fun. Just ask Ivy."

"Ivyyyyy!" Sparky squealed.

The kid looked around, but Ivy, of course, was nowhere in sight. The demon's lip started to quiver and tears poured down his face.

"Now ye made the wee bairn cry," Hob said. "Ye happy?"

"Oh, for the love of Mab," I muttered.

I ran a hand through my hair and looked up and down the rows of shabby market stalls and glaring neon signs. I'd brought our ragtag group to the main shopping street on Joysen Hill. The Hill was where all of the city's action was. You want girls, weapons, mind-bending potions, and magical portents? This was the place to be.

Harborsmouth's chamber of commerce had even hung banners across the street, promising visitors that they could find their thrill on Joysen Hill. The Hill was where tourists came to lose their wallets. Sometimes, they also lost their minds or their lives, but true entertainment always comes with a cost—all the good things in life do.

Joysen Hill had been a no-brainer.

Not so long ago, the demon kid had experienced an unfortunate incident with my cats, so the court of cats, for all its fun, wasn't an option. I'd toyed with the idea of going further up the hill to Sacred Heart Church to see Ivy's pal Galliel—what kid doesn't love a unicorn?—but realized Sparky wouldn't be able to enter holy ground.

Hob was another conundrum. The hearth brownie had recently lost his home and his place of employment when Madam Kaye's Magic Emporium was reduced to rubble. The Emporium's central location in Harborsmouth's Old Port Quarter meant no pub crawls through the cobblestone streets of the Quarter. The hearth brownie was grouchy enough without the looming reminder of all he'd recently lost.

Heading uptown was also out of the question. The troll kid's emo grunge look would never pass in the glitz and glitter of the city's business district, and Harborsmouth's parks were boring. Plus, the Cailleach Hag lived in Founders Park and that witch gave me the creeps.

"Fix this," Marvin said, stepping forward to loom over me.

The troll kid didn't scare me, but the sobbing demon on his shoulders had my eyes darting every which way, looking for any conceivable entertainment to distract Sparky. Ivy never said anything about crying kids.

I expanded my search, reaching out with my enhanced senses, considering various possibilities for mischief and mayhem. That was when I noticed the dancing slice of pizza. I tilted my head, scarred ears swiveling to catch the bizarre huckster's promises of food and fun.

"Come one, come all!" the dancing pizza shouted. "Eat, play, win fabulous prizes!"

Fabulous prizes, eh? That sounded promising. It didn't hurt that the diminutive demon's love for pizza was near legendary. The little tyke could put away an entire pie in seconds.

"Buck up, Sparky," I said, thrusting my shoulders back and tilting my head to smile at the demon. "I see pizza in your near future."

Sparky tugged at one of his long, floppy ears, his thumb in his mouth as he peeked past the safety of Marvin's large head. The troll raised an eyebrow, and I pasted a smile on my face. Who knows, this might actually be tolerable. In addition to pizza to eat, there was the promise of prizes to win. I always have been unnaturally good at games of chance.

I'm not just a pretty face.

I hastened my step, ignoring the less salubrious residents of the Hill as I swaggered toward the neon wonder that was Ratfink's Family Fun Palace.

"Pizzzaaa!" Sparky squealed and clapped his hands, catching sight of the dancing pizza slice.

The unusual tightness in my chest uncoiled. The kid was happy, and I'd found the perfect place to entertain my charges. The smug smile forming on my lips ended in a hiss as a scrawny, tattooed arm lunged out, barring my way into the gaming establishment.

I looked down at the small clawed hand on my chest and growled. The hand was attached to a six-foot-tall rat with a protruding belly, chipped yellowed teeth, and a patch over one eye. I glared at the wererat's beady good eye, extending my claws.

"Remove your hand, rat, or I'll remove it for you— permanently," I said.

I licked my lips and smiled.

"I'd grow it back, ye stupid cat," he said. The rat lifted his hand from my chest, and wiggled his claw-tipped fingers. "And the name's Roz. Ye want to make a complaint, take it up with the boss man."

He hooked a thumb over his sloping shoulder to the dark alcove where I assume his boss was hiding.

"I'm not here to eat you, not today and not if you play nice," I said. "We're here for the pizza and prizes. Unless you want to anger the lord of the cat sidhe?"

"You're the local cat sidhe lord?" he asked.

"Does anyone else look this good in leather pants?" I asked.

A multitude of painful, high-pitched squeaks came from the shadows behind the doorman, and he sighed.

"Guess tonight's your lucky night, cat lord," Roz said. "Boss man says you can come in, but you still gotta pay."

"And what kind of payment is Ratfink demanding?" I asked, narrowing my eyes.

Never trust a wererat, especially one who's survived long on Joysen Hill.

"Normal kind, for now," he said. "Two hundred in cash for four play passes. Ye get fifty back if you don't break anything. Consider it a safety deposit."

"Two hundred to enter this hovel?" I asked, sputtering in outrage.

I stepped forward, forcing the rat back a step. A rune-covered switchblade appeared in his hand. He used it to scratch at the bristly grey fur along the edge of his eye patch, and the threat was clear.

"Ye gotta pay to play," he said.

Any other time, I'd have gutted the man and made balloon animals with his intestines, but I had a bargain with Ivy Granger to keep her kids safe. Sparky started to sniffle, and I took a deep breath. I'd promised the kids a fun night on the town, and I always delivered on my promises.

I'd make this a night to remember.

I tossed over a bag of coins, and a smaller rat came waddling out of the shadows.

"Ah, very good, very good," he mumbled, eyes on the gold. "Welcome to Ratfink's Family Fun Palace."

"Ratfink, I presume?" I asked.

"Yes, yes, that's me, Ratfink's the name," he said, pumping my hand in his slippery, sweaty grasp.

I pulled away, wiping my hand on one of the threadbare velvet curtains that lined the doorway. The curtain's fleas probably had fleas, but anything was better than Ratfink's wormlike fingers and soft, sweaty palms.

If the corpulent wererat was offended, he didn't let on. Instead, he stroked his belly with tiny hands, letting out a high-pitch squeak-filled laugh. Funny, I didn't find being ripped off by a sleazeball wererat all that amusing.

"We paid your extortionate prices, Ratfink," I said, voice sharp as the multitude of small blades strapped to my body. "Let us in."

"Of course, of course, my dear man," he said, rocking on his heels. "But first, an important question, most important. Is it anyone's birthday?"

"Do the rat man be rabid, ye think?" Hob asked.

Marvin shrugged, and Sparky pointed at Roz and mouthed "pirate" much to the doorman's evident chagrin. I might have laughed if Ratfink hadn't let out a wheezing, sputtering gasp.

"Rabid?" he asked, tiny hands flailing. "No disease at Ratfink's Family Fun Palace, none at all, I can assure you. Only fun, and games, and *fabulous prizes.*"

"And pizza?" Marvin asked.

"Yes, man, of course," Ratfink said. He pulled back a curtain with a flourish. "That goes without saying, yes. The largest pizzas in Harborsmouth. Already in the guidebooks, we are. The best pizza on the Hill. Fast service too. Only the best, the best, my dear fellow."

Sparky's eyes widened, and Marvin's mouth hung open in surprise. Beyond the curtain was an assault on the senses that only a rat, or a child, could truly enjoy. The place was a claustrophobe's nightmare, a warren of brightly colored entertainment and gluttonous excess.

To our right hung oversized signs in every language, even the dead ones, announcing amazing, stupendous activities that seemed to include a dubious amount of climbing ropes and wading through pits of tiny balls. Down the middle, row upon row of games emitted the incessant clang of bells, claxon ring of alarms, and the strobing flash of lights. A bizarre dinner theater was located to our left, the cloying scent of oregano heavy on the air.

"Not exactly a palace," I muttered.

"Ah, but there is a palace," Ratfink said, waddling forward. "Earn enough tickets and you can go inside the bouncy palace."

"Now would be a good time to remind 'em of the rules," Roz said, tapping his switchblade at a brightly lit sign on the wall.

"Yes, yes, the rules, most important," Ratfink said. "Do follow the rules. And, here are your passes. Don't lose them. These are your passports to fun."

I wrinkled my nose, extending my claws as I reached for our passes. Ratfink disappeared behind his curtain, and Roz read off the rules.

"No food in the ball pit," he said. "No pukin' in the bouncy palace. No heckling the happy fun time sing along heads. Absolutely positively no refunds."

I frowned, raising an eyebrow.

"What the devil is a happy fun time sing along head?" I asked.

"You'll find out soon enough," Roz said.

And with that ominous prediction, he closed the curtain, leaving me with three bug-eyed companions.

"Come on, let's get you that pizza," I said, sauntering to the dinner theater.

Maybe this wouldn't be so bad. The kids were speechless and the pizza was served in a more subdued part of the establishment. I might just survive the experience.

That's when a hundred grinning undead animals thrust their heads through the walls and began to sing.

"Oberon's great silver balls," I muttered, dropping into a booth and grabbing a menu to hide behind.

The undead animals had sewn on smiles and milky dead eyes, but they could sure belt out show tunes and they murdered that Ratfink's Family Fun Palace jingle.

"They be dead," Hob said, blinking at the ghoulish singing animals. "This be somethin' wee ones like?"

I shook my head. I'd seen a lot in my nine lives, but nothing so strange as Ratfink's and its tone-deaf taxidermied talent, and something told me we'd only just scratched the surface.

"Most likely a cost saving measure," I said, warily keeping an eye on the creepy critters as Marvin and Sparky scanned the menu. The demon was bouncing to the music, legs kicking the vinyl bench in time to the beat. "Everybody want pizza?"

"Did somebody say PIZZA?"

I had to grab the table to keep from jumping. The voice came from a werepanda, on roller skates. She'd zoomed up to us and was gnawing on her pen like it was a bamboo stalk, waiting to take our order.

"Pizzzaaa!" Sparky squealed.

"Dinner or dessert?" she asked, chomping on her pen.

"What does it matter?" I asked.

"Dinner pizza has sauce and cheese and dessert pizza has cinnamon and sugar," she said with the long suffering sigh of someone who gets asked the same question a million times a night.

"We'll take four dinner pizzas and two dessert pizzas for the kids and a stiff drink for me," I said.

"Abracadabra, enjoy your meal," she said, steaming food appearing on the table. "Don't take any food in the ball pit and no puking in the bouncy palace. Bon appétit."

With that unpalatable pronouncement, the waitress skated away and my charges fell on their meals like, well, a hungry demon, troll, and brownie.

I pushed my food away, letting the kids have it, and wandered toward the kitchen. Curiosity is an affliction that often proves fatal to my kind, but I couldn't resist a peek. The restaurant's teleportation of hot food from the kitchen to our table was a handy trick.

I liked tricks, the sneakier the better.

With a quick glance up and down the restaurant, I pushed into the kitchen. The swinging doors squeaked behind me and I winced. I'd planned on sauntering in and charming the information out of the waitress or perhaps a buxom line cook. I hadn't bargained for the sea of pleading faces.

Dozens of diminutive faeries, mostly hobgoblins and hinkypunk, turned gaunt, grime-covered wide-eyed faces my way, chains rattling where the iron dragged along the greasy kitchen floor. Some bowed their heads, averting their eyes, but most stared at me, their pale faces and feverish eyes painfully bright above iron collars.

"Well, I'll be a bugbear's uncle," I muttered.

"Please, sir," a female goblin cried out, an infant held to her chest. "Please, help us."

I stepped forward, grimacing. This was going to sting a bit. I grabbed a grimy dishcloth and wrapped it around my hand, but the iron still penetrated the cloth and skin, leaving behind a deep, gnawing ache. I savored the pain, and made it a promise, one that would return to Ratfink and his flunkies in spades.

Using my enhanced speed and feline reflexes, I freed the kitchen slaves in minutes. The faeries were already heading for the delivery entrance, making their escape, when Hob burst through the swinging doors at my back.

"Ye better come quick," he said. "The little lad's in trouble."

Hob rushed out the doors, stubby legs a blur of motion as he ran through the restaurant toward the gaming area beyond.

"I've barely been gone ten minutes," I said, yelling over the incessant whir and clank of gaming machines. "Sparky was eating when I left. What trouble could he possibly get up to?"

"Ye know that rule 'bout no food in the ball pit?" he asked. He came to a stop at an enormous aquarium tank filled with brightly colored balls, and put a finger to the side of his nose.

"Let me guess," I said, eyes scanning the tank. "The kid brought his bloody food in the ball pit."

"Got it in one, cat lord," Roz said, stepping out to block my path.

"Octopuuusss!" Sparky squealed.

I whipped my head toward the tank, eyes widening. Now I knew why food wasn't allowed in the ball pit.

"That's no octopus," I said with a hiss. "What is that thing?"

Tentacles writhed through the balls, suction cups the size of my head clinging to the aquarium glass as the creature pulled itself along.

"It don't matter," Roz said, switchblade opening with a snick of metal on metal. "You break the rules, you pay the price."

"Another time, Roz," I said. "Looks like my dance card is full."

Roz lunged forward, leading with the switchblade, and I deflected easily with my claws, pushing his arm wide. Instead of maneuvering around the wererat, I dove inside his guard, and head-butted his face hard enough to break his nose. Cartilage crunched, and I smiled, licking my lips.

"Hob!" I yelled, tossing a knife to the hearth brownie.

The blade was a sword in the tiny faerie's hands, but he didn't fumble. He ran up the ball pit stairs and I followed, pushing aside the ignorant humans who couldn't see the monsters in their midst.

Foolish humans tricked by glamour could be amusing, but Ratfink was using the gifts of enslaved fae for his own profits. More than that, if the enormous tentacles were any indication, he had somehow captured an elder god and was offering it the city's children as sacrifice, probably to provide the kind of spell that kept this place off the local Hunters' Guild's radar. There was no art to this con, no finesse. Just a rat with a festering heart and a greedy belly, made fat by the suffering of the Hill's weak and less fortunate.

I climbed the stairs four at a time, my catlike reflexes always finding purchase in the small shadowed spaces between customers. At the top, chaos reigned.

Marvin was barreling parents over to save their children, pulling kids from the ball pit and pushing them away from the aquarium's edge. Children cried and parents screamed, but they couldn't see the hungry monster with its writhing tentacles and gaping maw. They treated Marvin as if he were the monster, ruining their family night.

I'd seen enough.

I dove into the pit, grabbed Sparky, plunking him on the astroturf-covered platform that surrounded the tank. The kid laughed, and I had to grin.

"You having fun?" I asked.

"Octopuuusss!" he squealed.

I shook my head, trying not to laugh.

"Leave the octopus to me," I said. "I got a job for you, kid. Are you up to it?"

The demon tilted his head, one floppy ear covered in sauce that smelled suspiciously of oregano. He'd probably eaten an entire pizza while I'd been freeing faeries in the kitchen, and, judging from the sticky crust protruding from his pockets, had stashed away dessert for later.

"Job?" he asked.

"Go pull that fire alarm over there," I said. "Then wait for me or Marvin or Hob. Don't go back in the ball pit. Okay?"

Sparky nodded, but instead of pulling the fire alarm, he caught the nearest staff member on fire. That'd do. The wererat's cheap polyester uniform went up in flames, and the fire alarm started to trill.

The humans stopped fighting Marvin and ran for the doors, but not every kid was out of the tank. A tentacle rose above the center of the tank, a little girl in its rubbery grip. The balls nearest me vibrated, scraping against each other as something enormous moved more fully into this world, displacing the balls and cracking the aquarium tank.

The elder god was hungry, so I filled him full of iron. With a claw and a prayer, I tore a hole in the fabric of reality between the ball pit and the kitchen. A pile of cast off iron chains and shackles came tumbling into the creature's maw.

With an ear-popping pressure change, I let go and let reality snap back into place. I'd have one hell of a headache tomorrow, and I'd be weak as a kitten for days, but the gambit worked. The tentacle loosened and I caught the falling girl. I was handing her to Marvin when a great gurgling began at my back.

Marvin's eyes widened, and we ran. I grabbed Hob and Sparky, ignoring the brownie's grumbled threats, and leapt down the stairs and across the gaming floor. Another gurgle rumbled and the entire building shook.

"Get down!" I shouted.

We dove for cover behind a line of arcade games, barely avoiding shards of glass and projectile gelatinous goo. The little girl squirmed out of Marvin's arms and ran to a confused looking man standing by the exit. The two humans stumbled out the door, which just left us, the remaining staff, and the whirring arcade games splattered and dripping with pink and grey flesh.

I don't think I'll be getting that safety deposit back.

I wiped elder god from my shoulder, and grinned at my companions.

"Anyone want cotton candy?" I asked, spying the roller skating werepanda now working the cotton candy booth.

The candy was spun by spiderfae and was probably the safest thing to eat in a wererat's establishment. Which was good since we each ate three huge clusters of the stuff.

Sparky let out a happy burp, and I nudged him with my elbow.

"Let's go hit the bouncy palace," I said. "First one to puke gets to pick where we go next."

Breaking Ratfink's rules was fun. I should have come here ages ago. Pesky elder god and his illusion spells.

"Ye mean we're not a goin' back to the loft?" Hob asked.

"No way," I said, leaning forward and rubbing my hands together.

When you've lived as long as I have, it's hard to find anything new and interesting. But hanging with these kids? Saving helpless faeries from enslavement and sweatshop conditions? That was a whole new kind of mischief and mayhem, and we had all of Joysen Hill to tackle.

"We're just getting started."

IVY GRANGER WORLD

The world of Ivy Granger includes the Ivy Granger Psychic Detective series and the Hunters' Guild series.

Don't miss these great books set in the world of Ivy Granger.

Available in Ebook, Trade Paperback, and Audiobook.

GET LOST IN TRANSLATIONS

Books in the world of Ivy Granger are now available in multiple languages!

Now you can read your favorite urban fantasy series in English, Dutch, German, Italian, Afrikaans, Portuguese, French, and Spanish.

Visit EJStevensAuthor.com for more information.

SHADOW SIGHT

Welcome to Harborsmouth, where monsters walk the streets unseen by humans...except those with second sight, like Ivy Granger.

Ivy Granger's second sight is finally giving her life purpose. Ivy and her best friend Jinx may not be raking in the dough, but their psychic detective agency pays the bills—most of the time. Their only worry is the boredom of a slow day and the occasional crazy client—until a demon walks through their door.

Demons are never a good sign.

BLOOD AND MISTLETOE: AN IVY GRANGER NOVELLA

Holidays are worse than a full moon for making people crazy. In Harborsmouth, where many of the residents are undead vampires or monstrous fae, the combination may prove deadly.

Holidays are Hell, a point driven home when a certain demon attorney returns with information regarding a series of bloody murders. Five Harborsmouth residents have been killed and every victim has one thing in common—they are fae. Whoever is killing faeries must be stopped, but they only leave one clue behind—a piece of mistletoe floating in a pool of the victim's blood.

The holidays just got interesting.

GHOST LIGHT

*Holidays are worse than a full moon for making people crazy.
In Harborsmouth, where many of the residents are undead
vampires or monstrous fae, the combination may prove deadly.*

Ivy Granger is back, gathering clues in the darkest shadows of
downtown Harborsmouth. With the lives of multiple clients on
the line, she's in a race against time. Ivy finally has a lead to
the whereabouts of the one person who can help her control her
wisp abilities, but will she put the needs of her clients above
her own?

If Ivy doesn't find a solution soon, she could wind up a ghost
herself.

CLUB NEXUS: AN IVY GRANGER NOVELLA

A demon, an Unseelie faerie, and a vampire walk into a bar...

This Ivy Granger series novella contains four intertwining stories ICED, DUSTED, JINXED, and DEMONIZED set in Club Nexus, the hidden haunt of Harborsmouth's paranormal underworld.

BURNING BRIGHT

Burning down the house...

Ivy must rid the city of imps, keep Jinx from murdering her one solid link to Hell, and fulfill her bargain with the Green Lady—with sidhe assassins hot on her tail.

BIRTHRIGHT

Being a faerie princess isn't all it's cracked up to be.

Ivy must go to Faerie, but the gateway to the Wisp Court is through Tech Duinn, the house of Donn—Celtic god of the dead. Just her luck.

Ivy Granger thought she left the worst of Mab's creations behind when she escaped Faerie. She thought wrong.

In a cruel twist of fate, Ivy has unleashed a powerful horde of Unseelie beasts upon her city, turning her homecoming into a potential slaughter of innocents. Now Ivy must gather her allies to fight a reputedly unstoppable force—The Wild Hunt.

The only thing worse than being a Hunter in the fae-ridden city of Harborsmouth, is hunting vampires in Bruges.

With a desire to prove herself, protect the innocent, and advance within the ranks of the Hunters' Guild, Jenna Lehane hits the cobbled streets of Bruges with blades at the ready.

COMING SOON

Blood Rite

Ivy Granger psychic detective takes on a simple grave robbing case, but in Harborsmouth nothing is ever simple when dealing with the dead.

Watertight

When Torn is accused of murdering a local mermaid, Ivy Granger is plunged into the deep end of water fae politics.

With her psychic gifts and newfound wisp powers, locating Torn's alibi should be simple. Too bad a deadly enemy with a score to settle is lurking in Harborsmouth's darkest waters.

Ivy Granger might be in over her head. Even with the help of her kelpie king fiance, Ivy only has until the next high tide to prove Torn's innocence. With the clock counting down and the bodies piling up, Ivy better hope she finds an alibi that's watertight.

Dressed in White

On the eve of Jinx and Ivy's double wedding, a sinister figure is terrorizing Harborsmouth.

When reports of a homicidal jilted bride threaten their wedding plans, Ivy and Forneus set out to put a stop to the string of heinous acts. What they discover might just send the faerie and demon straight to Hell, and set Ivy on a path to rectify more than one evil deed.

Will Ivy tie the knot with her kelpie king, or will she be saying "I do" to the king of Hell? Her father's curse is on the line, and lives hang in the balance. No pressure.

PRAISE FOR THE WORLD OF IVY GRANGER

"Stevens draws you in instantly with well-developed and likeable characters."
-Ted Fauster, author of the World of Faerel series

"Move over Harry Dresden fans, Ivy Granger is here."
-Kelly Abell, author of the Haunted Destiny series

"I haven't met an Ivy Granger story I didn't like. ...I love a good Urban Fantasy and the Ivy Granger series is not just good it's great."
-James A. Moore, Bram Stoker Award nominated author of the Seven Forges series

"If you're a fan of Kim Harrison or Patricia Briggs kind of Urban Fantasy then you will love the Ivy Granger series."
-The Keeper Shelf

"E.J. Stevens did a great job creating a unique Urban Fantasy world."
-Parajunkee

"There is romance, action, mystery, plenty of things that go bump in the night, all told with humor and style."
-Paranormal Romance Guild

"Stevens has done a fantastic job with bringing her world to us."
-Urban Fantasy Investigations

"Want a clever, fun and unique Urban Fantasy? This is the series to check out."
-The Jeep Diva

"The Ivy Granger Series is fantastic!"
-Book Bite Reviews

IVY GRANGER FREEBIES

Get free Ivy Granger ringtones, wallpapers, audio samples and more at EJStevensAuthor.com.

E.J. Stevens is the author of the HUNTERS' GUILD urban fantasy series, the SPIRIT GUIDE young adult series, and the award-winning IVY GRANGER urban fantasy series. She is known for filling pages with quirky characters, bloodsucking vampires, psychotic faeries, and snarky, kick-butt heroines.

BTS Red Carpet Award winner for Best Novel, SYAE Award finalist for Best Paranormal, Best Horror, and Best Novella, winner of the PRG Reviewer's Choice Award for Best Paranormal Fantasy Novel, Best Young Adult Paranormal Series, Best Urban Fantasy Novel, and finalist for Best Young Adult Paranormal Novel and Best Urban Fantasy Series.

When E.J. isn't at her writing desk, she enjoys dancing along seaside cliffs, singing in graveyards, and sleeping in faerie circles. E.J. currently resides in a magical forest on the coast of Maine where she finds daily inspiration for her writing.

CONNECT WITH E.J. STEVENS

Twitter: @EJStevensAuthor
Website: www.EJStevensAuthor.com
Blog: www.FromtheShadows.info

www.ingramcontent.com/pod-product-compliance
Lightning Source LLC
Chambersburg PA
CBHW051509170626
46811CB00002B/725